CLONE WARS
ADVENTURES
VOLUME 4

STAR WARS®

CLONE WARS
ADVENTURES

VOLUME 4

ANOTHER FINE MESS
script and art The Fillbach Brothers
colors Pamela Rambo

THE BRINK
script Justin Lambros
art Rick Lacy
colors Dan Jackson

ORDERS
script Ryan Kaufman
art The Fillbach Brothers
colors Ronda Pattison

DESCENT
script Haden Blackman
art The Fillbach Brothers
colors Dave Nestelle

lettering
Michael David Thomas

cover
The Fillbach Brothers and Dan Jackson

Dark Horse Books®

visit us at www.abdopublishing.com

Reinforced library bound edition published in 2011 by Spotlight,
a division of the ABDO Group, 8000 West 78th Street, Edina, Minnesota 55439.
Spotlight produces high-quality reinforced library bound editions for schools and
libraries. Published by agreement with Dark Horse Comics, Inc., and Lucasfilm Ltd.
Printed in the United States of America, Melrose Park, Illinois.
052010
092010

This book contains at least 10% recycled materials.

Special thanks to Sue Rostoni, Leland Chee, and Amy Gary at Lucas Licensing

Cataloging-in-Publication Data

The Fillbach Brothers.
Star wars: clone wars adventures. Volume 4 / script and art the Fillback Brothers ;
colors, Pamela Rambo ; lettering, Michael David Thomas ;
cover art the Fillbach brothers and Dan Jackson.
Clone wars adventures -- Reinforced library bound ed.
p. cm. -- (Star Wars: Clone wars adventures)
1. Star Wars fiction--Comic books, strips, etc. 2. Graphic novels.
I. Rambo, Pamela. II. Thomas, Michael David. III. Title. IV. Title.
V. Title: Star Wars, Clone wars (Television program) VI. Series.
PN6728.S73 2004
741.5'973--dc22
ISBN 978-1-59961-907-1 (reinforced library bound edition)

All Spotlight books are reinforced library binding
and manufactured in the United States of America.

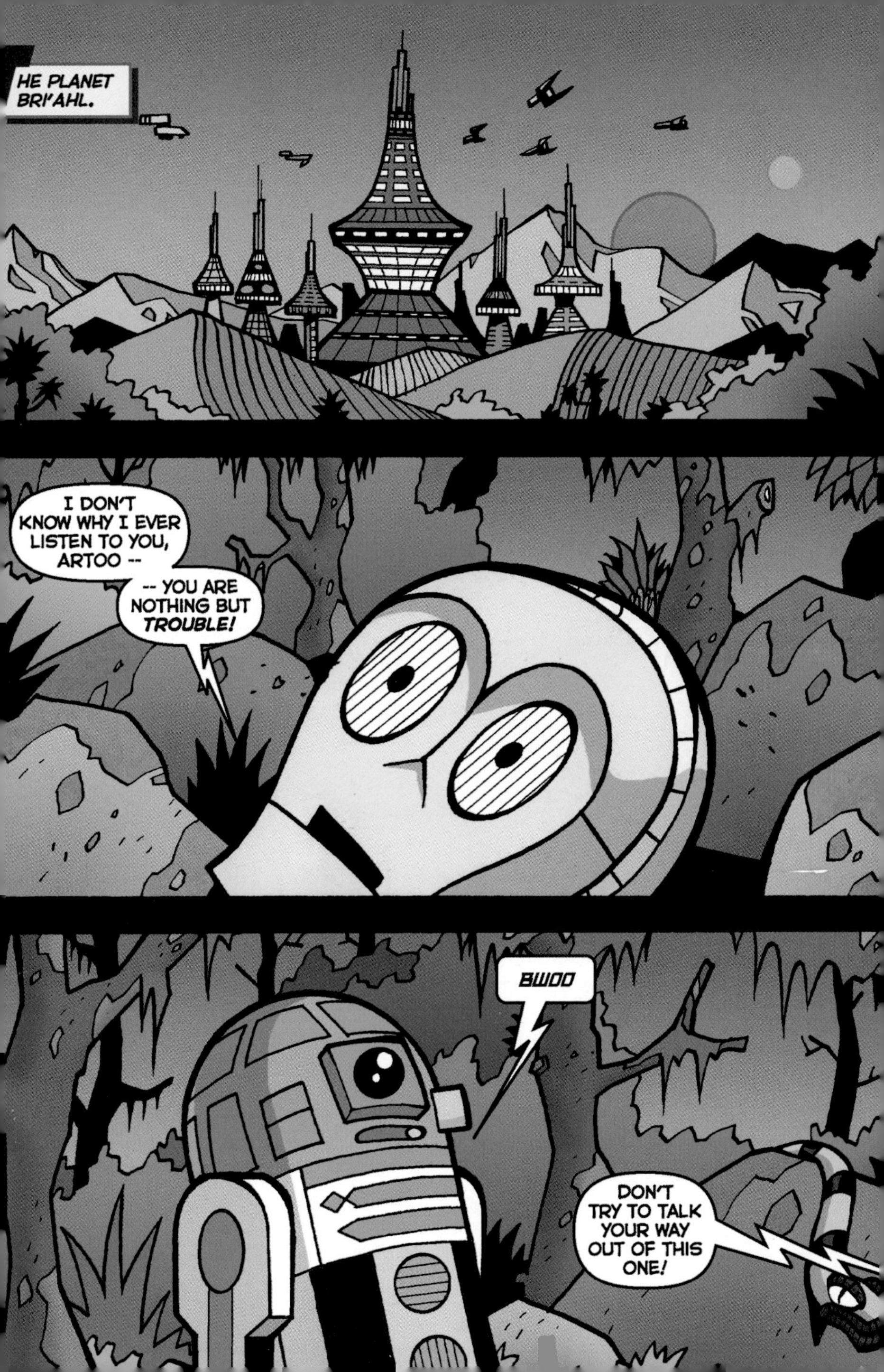
HE PLANET BRI'AHL.
I DON'T KNOW WHY I EVER LISTEN TO YOU, ARTOO --
-- YOU ARE NOTHING BUT *TROUBLE!*
BWOO
DON'T TRY TO TALK YOUR WAY OUT OF THIS ONE!

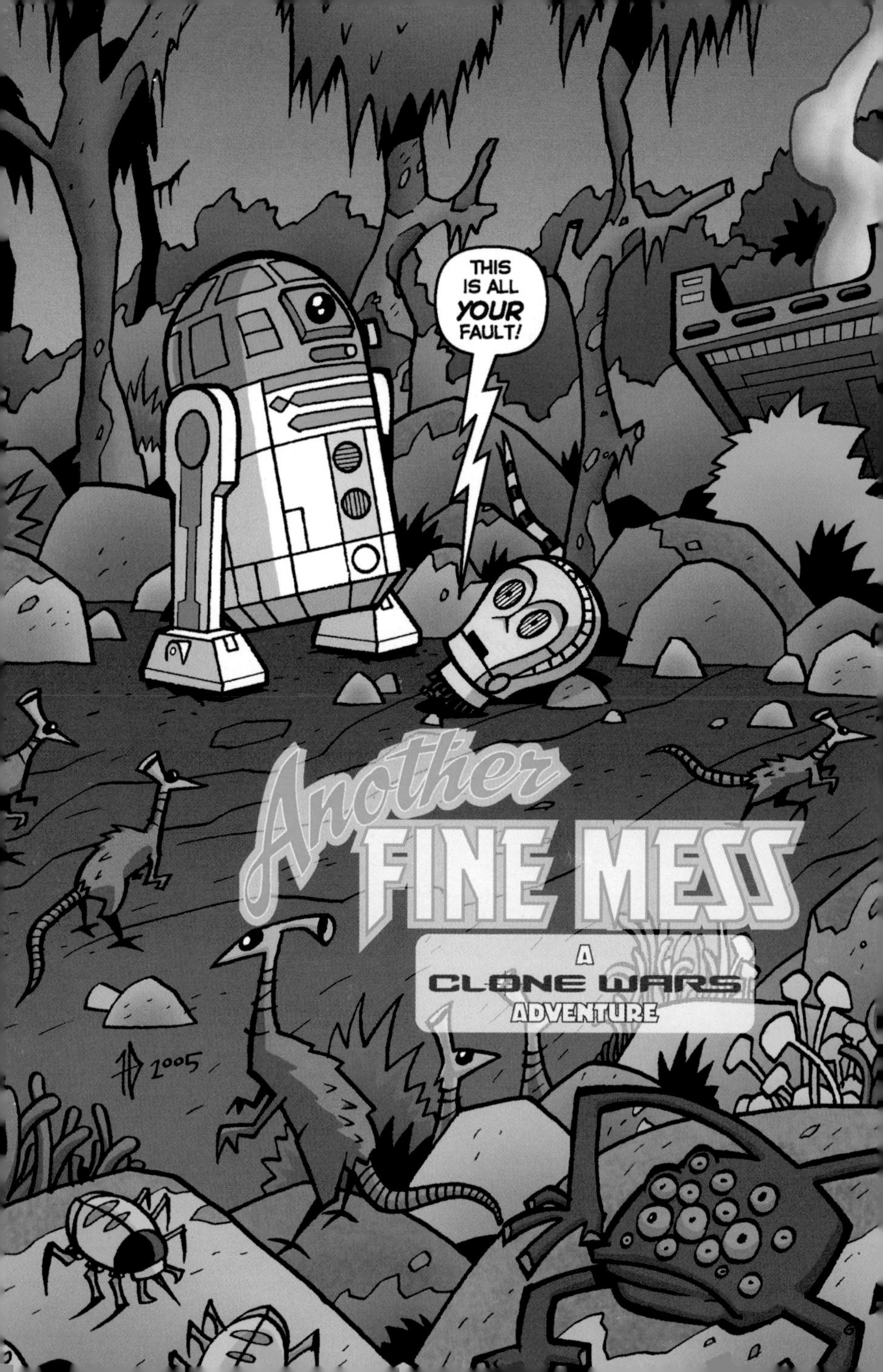
THIS IS ALL YOUR FAULT!
Another
FINE MESS
A
CLONE WARS
ADVENTURE
2005

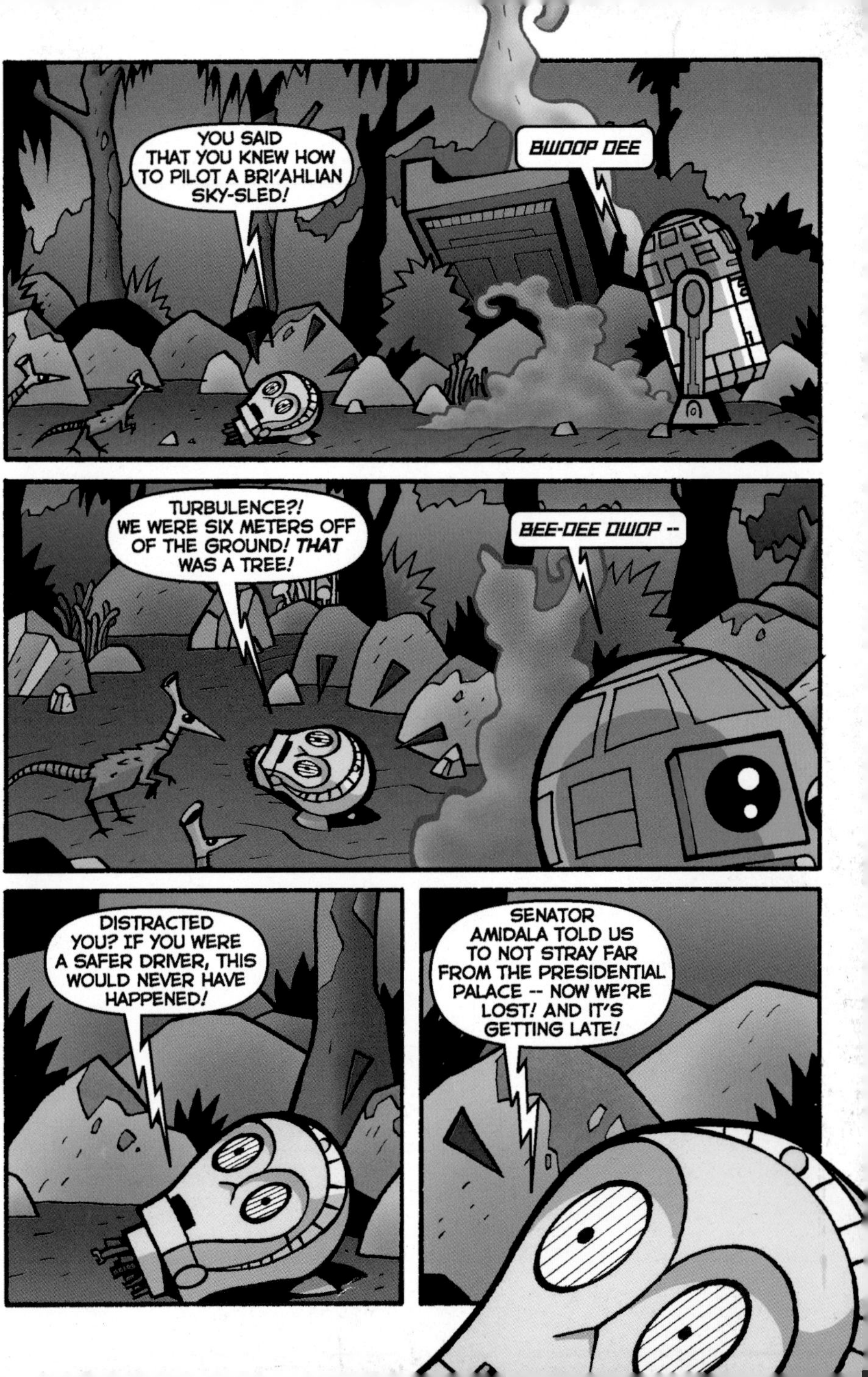
YOU SAID THAT YOU KNEW HOW TO PILOT A BRI'AHLIAN SKY-SLED!
BWOOP DEE
TURBULENCE?! WE WERE SIX METERS OFF OF THE GROUND! THAT WAS A TREE!
BEE-DEE DWOP --
DISTRACTED YOU? IF YOU WERE A SAFER DRIVER, THIS WOULD NEVER HAVE HAPPENED!
SENATOR AMIDALA TOLD US TO NOT STRAY FAR FROM THE PRESIDENTIAL PALACE -- NOW WE'RE LOST! AND IT'S GETTING LATE!

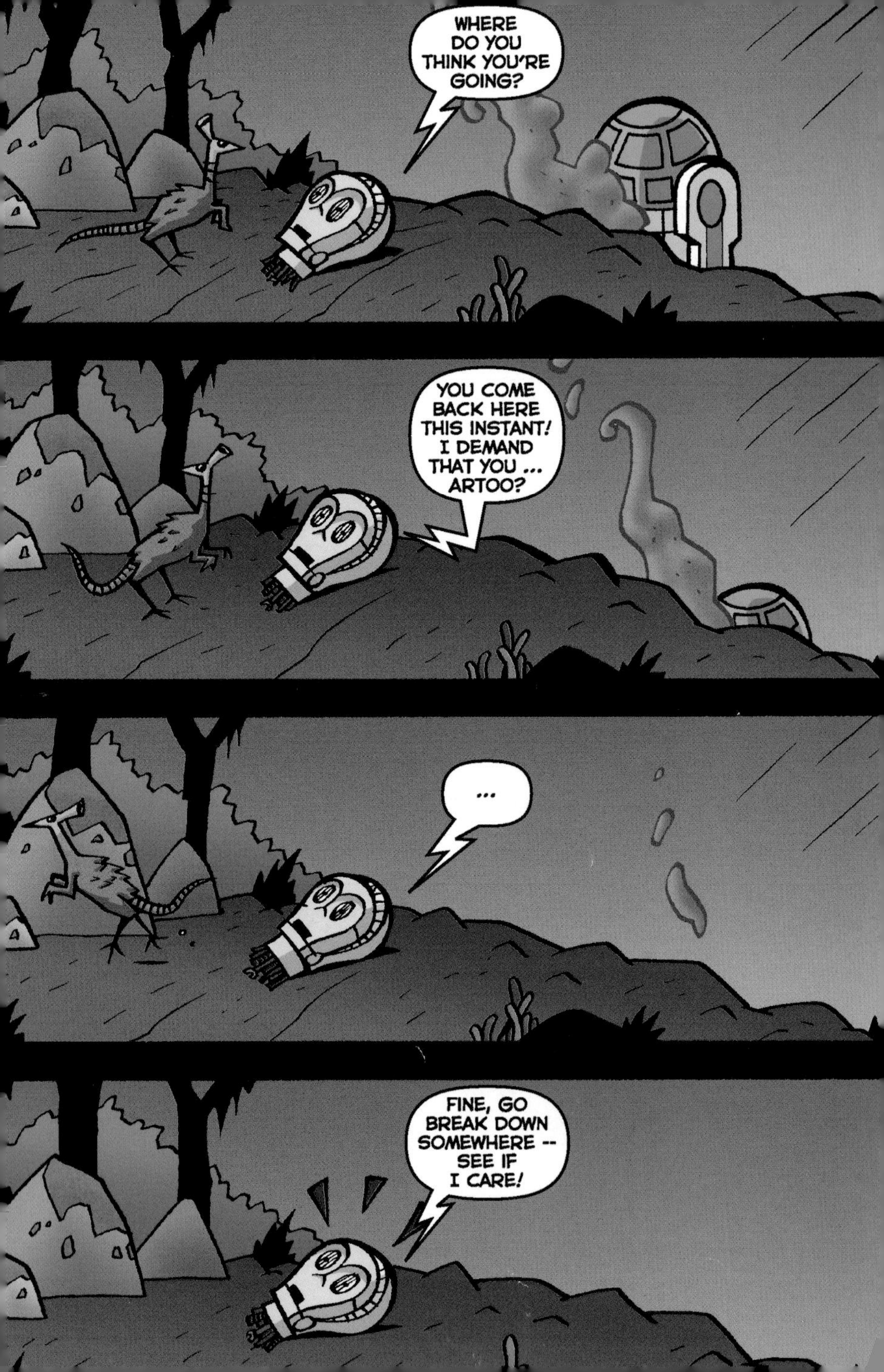
WHERE DO YOU THINK YOU'RE GOING?
YOU COME BACK HERE THIS INSTANT! I DEMAND THAT YOU ... ARTOO?
...
FINE, GO BREAK DOWN SOMEWHERE -- SEE IF I CARE!

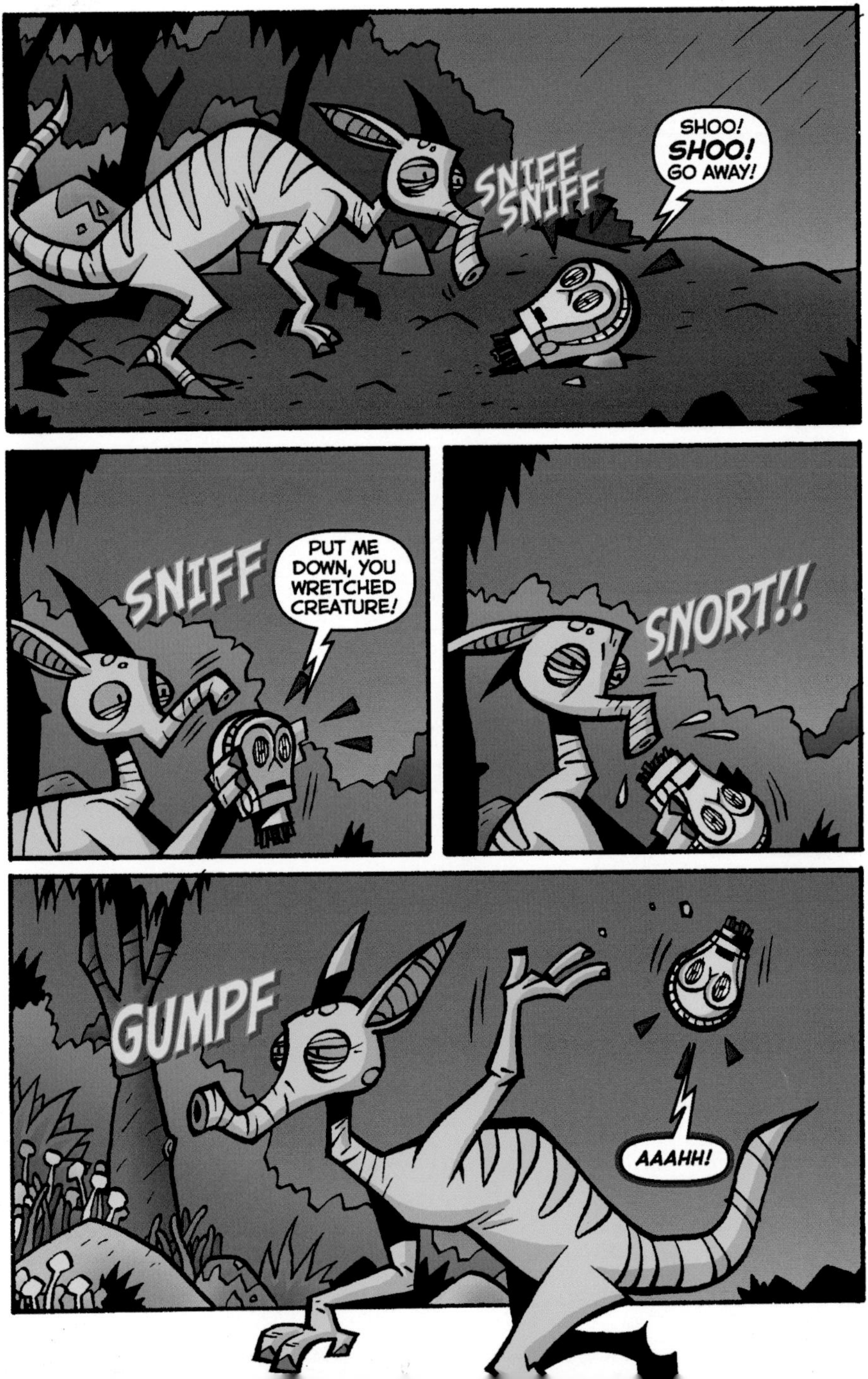
SNIFF SNIFF
SHOO! SHOO! GO AWAY!
SNIFF
PUT ME DOWN, YOU WRETCHED CREATURE!
SNORT!!
GUMPF
AAAHH!

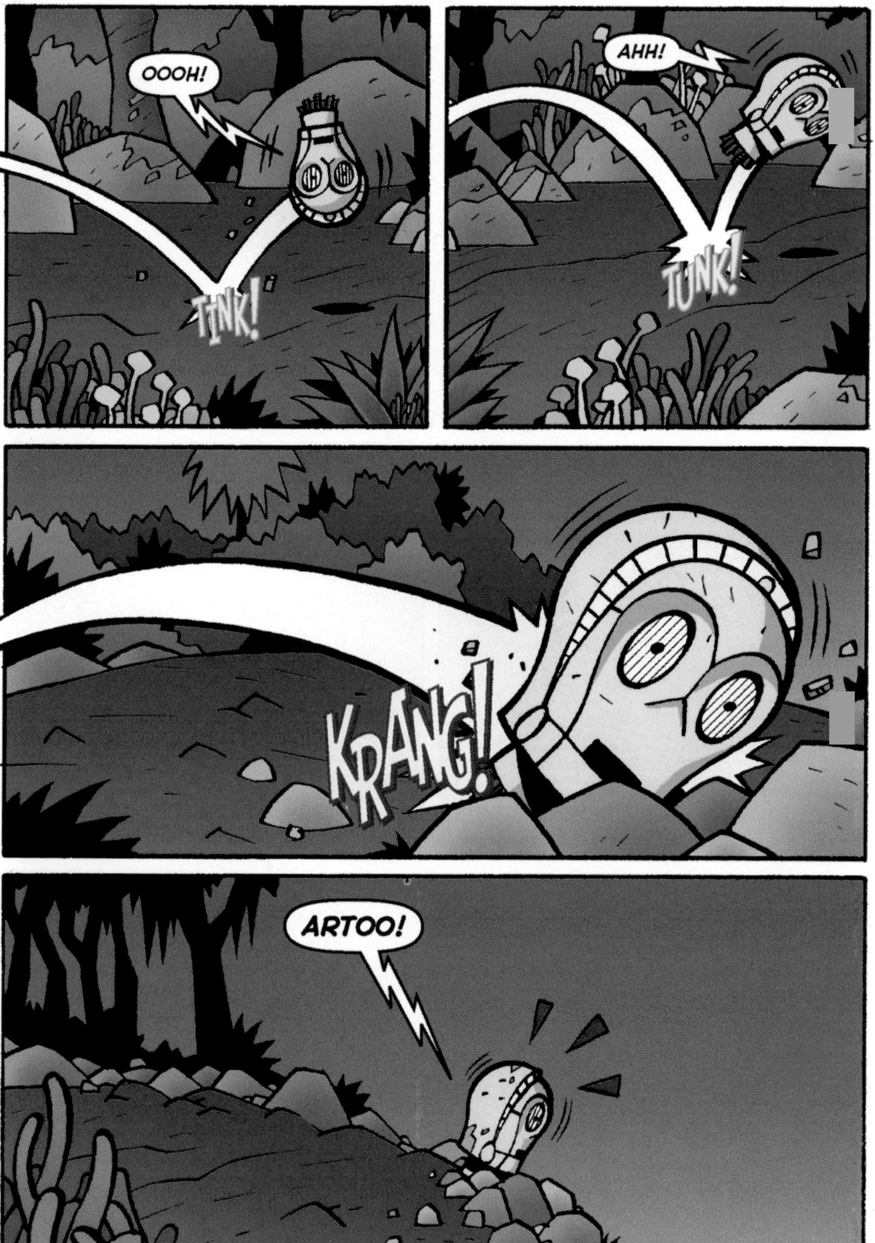
OOOH!
TINK!
AHH!
TUNK!
KRANG!
ARTOO!

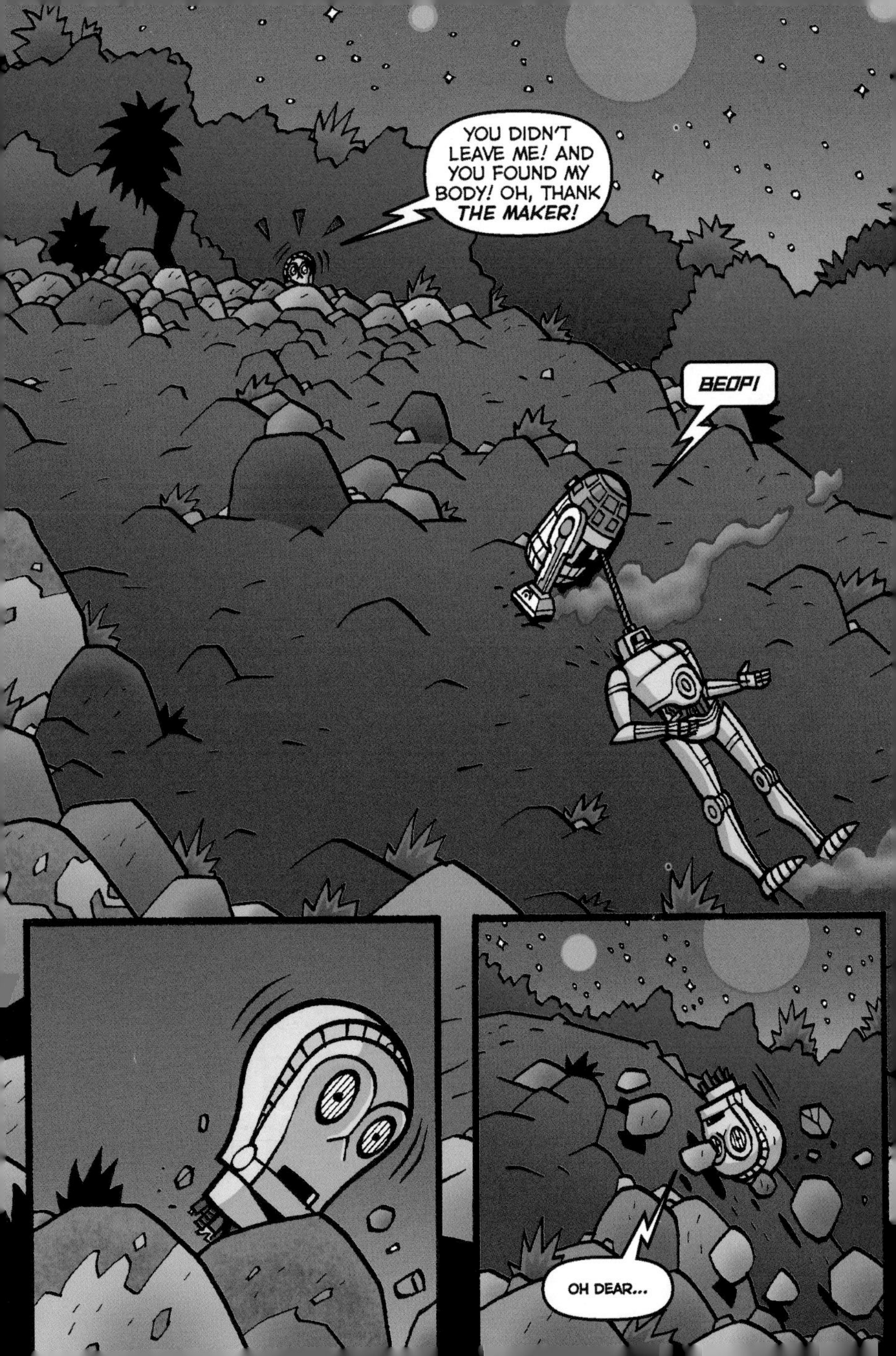
YOU DIDN'T LEAVE ME! AND YOU FOUND MY BODY! OH, THANK THE MAKER!
BEEP!
OH DEAR...

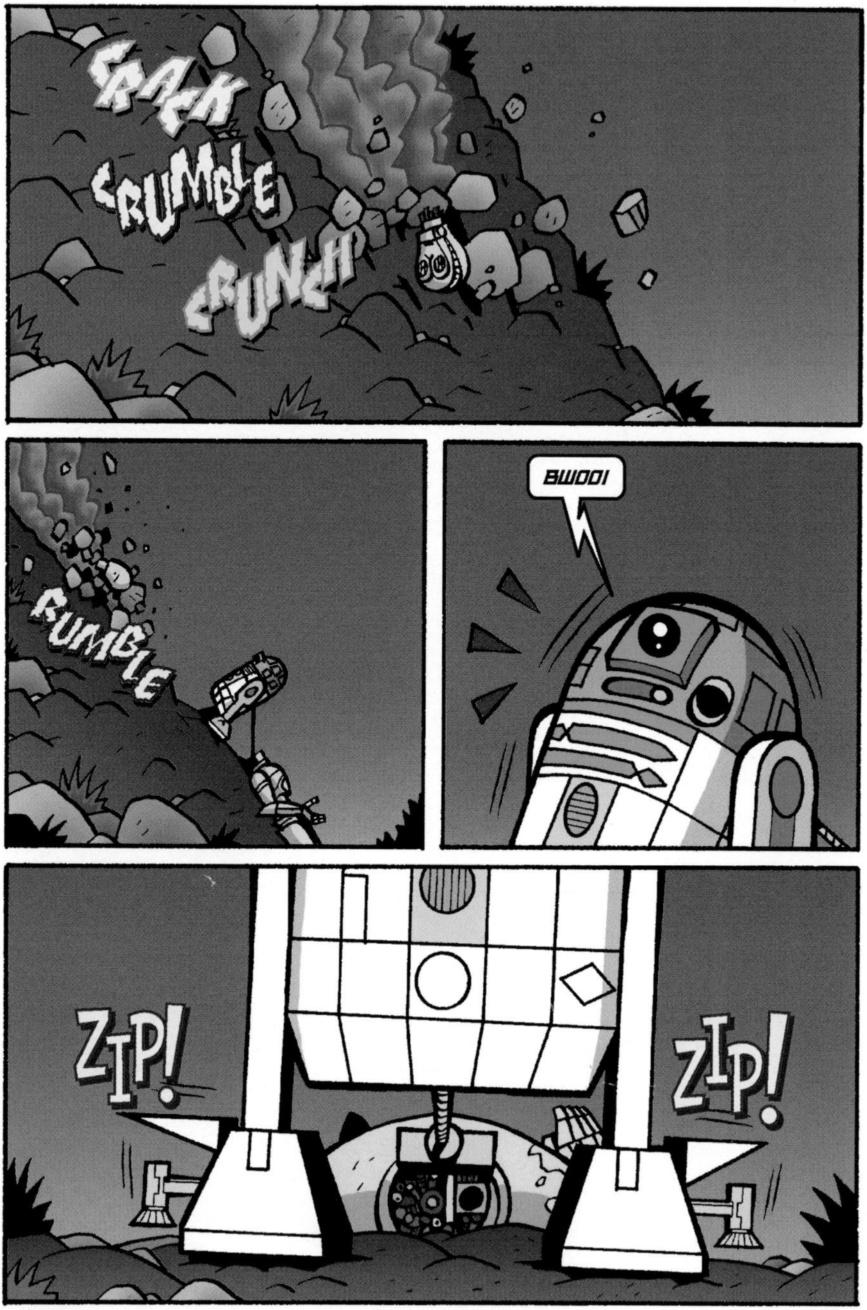
CRACK
CRUMBLE
CRUNCH
RUMBLE
BWOO!
ZIP!
ZIP!

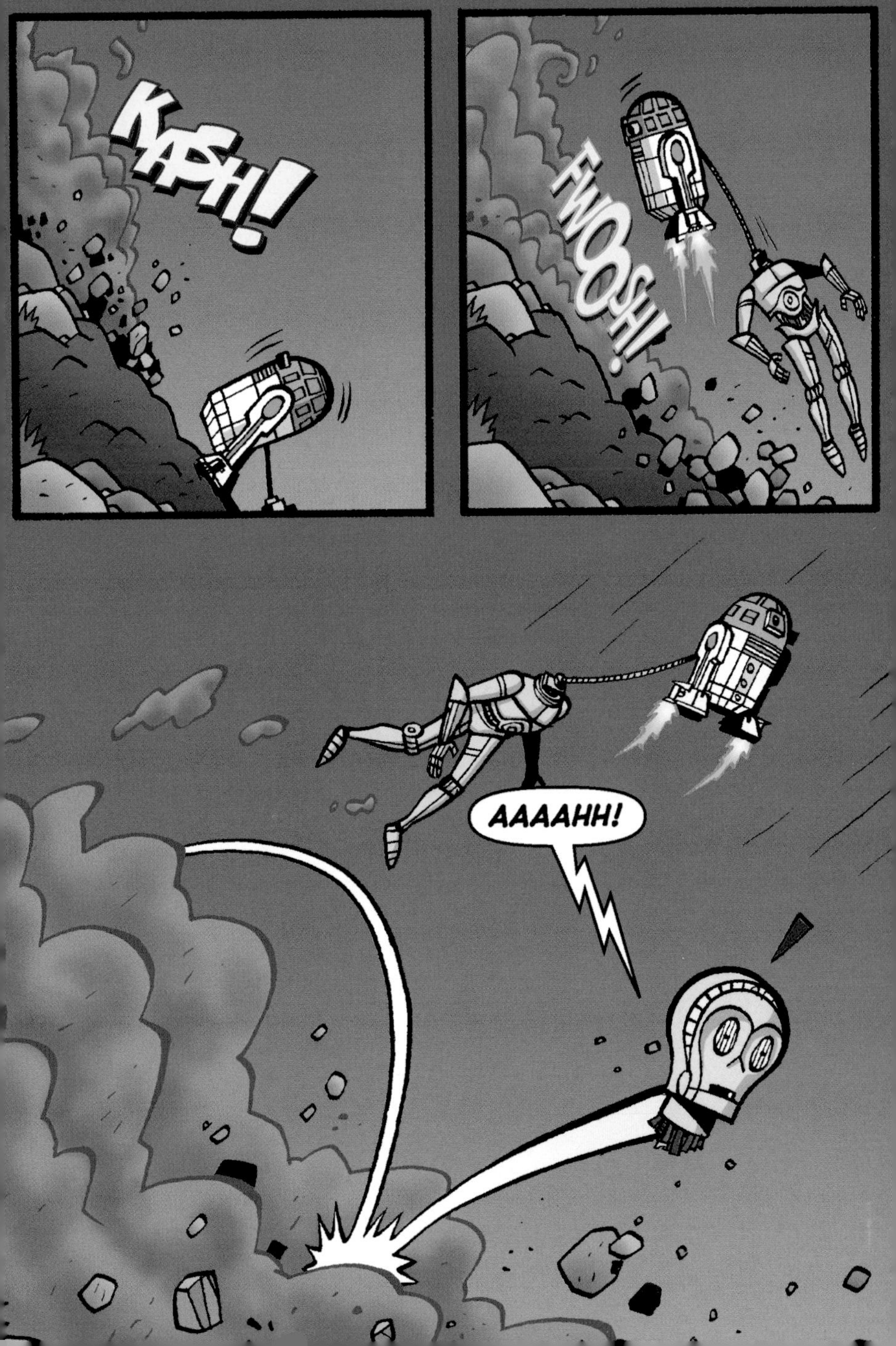
KASH!
FWOOSH!!
AAAAHH!

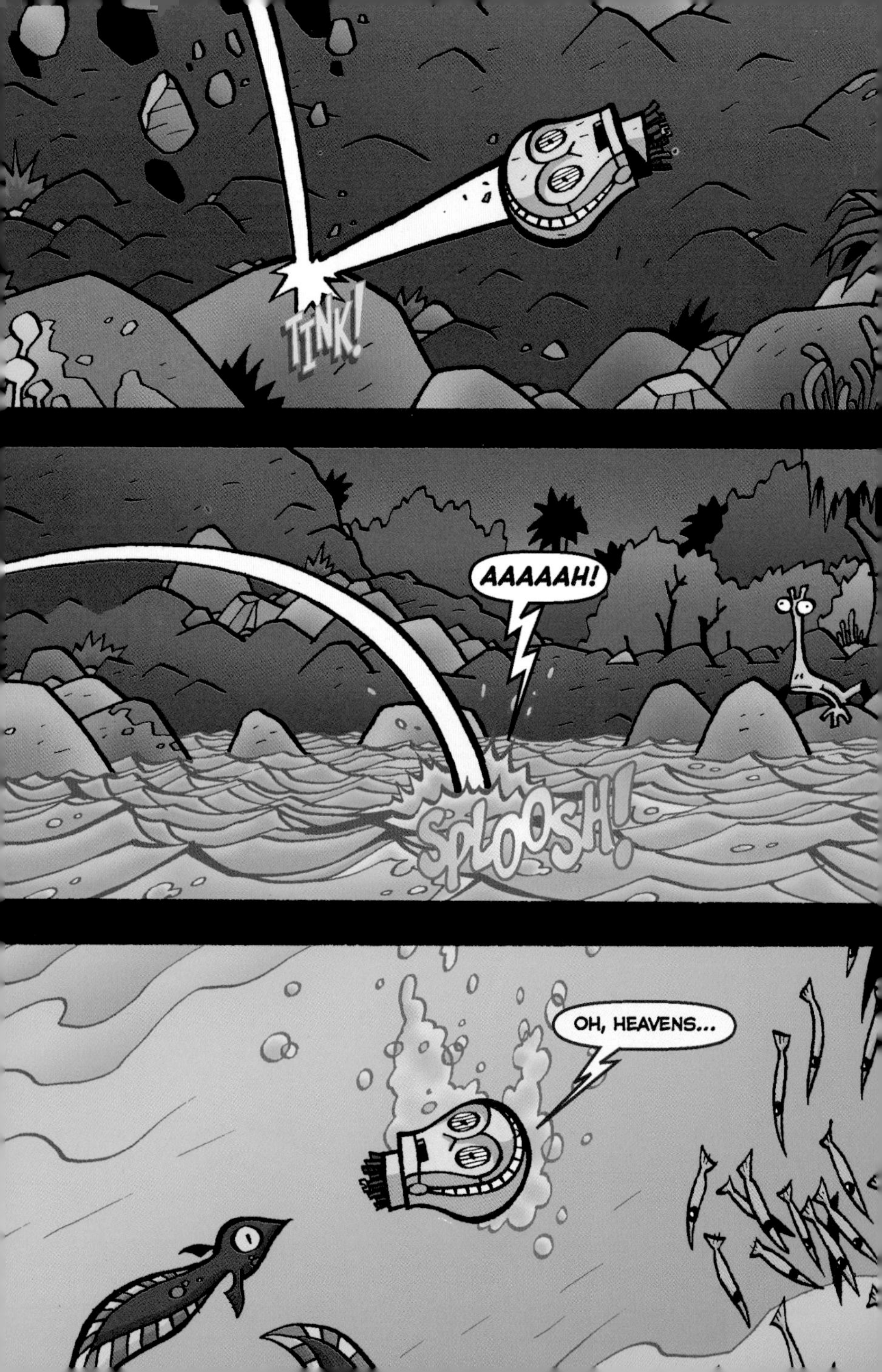
TINK!
AAAAAH!
SPLOOSH!
OH, HEAVENS...

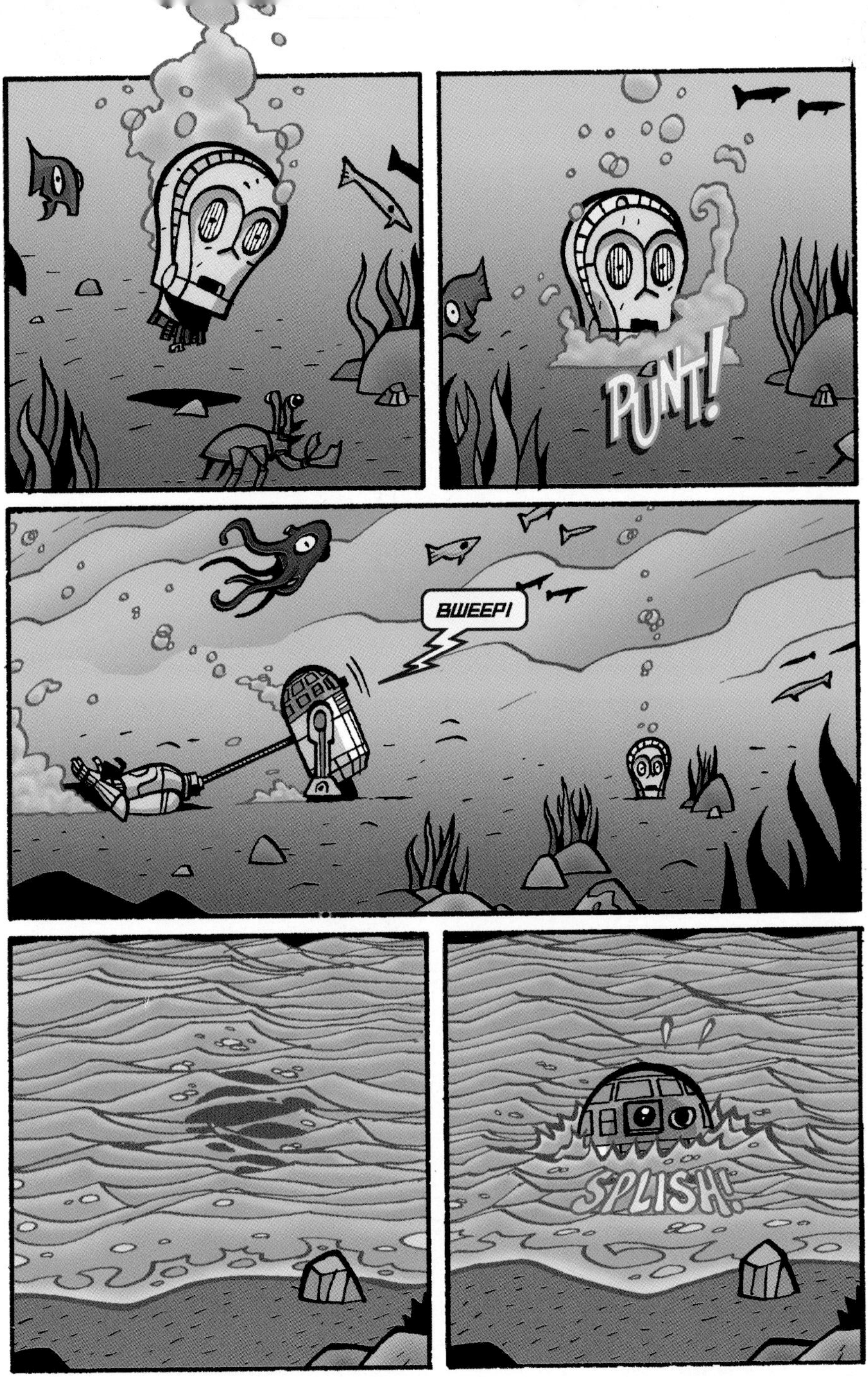
PUNT!
BWEEP!
SPLISH!

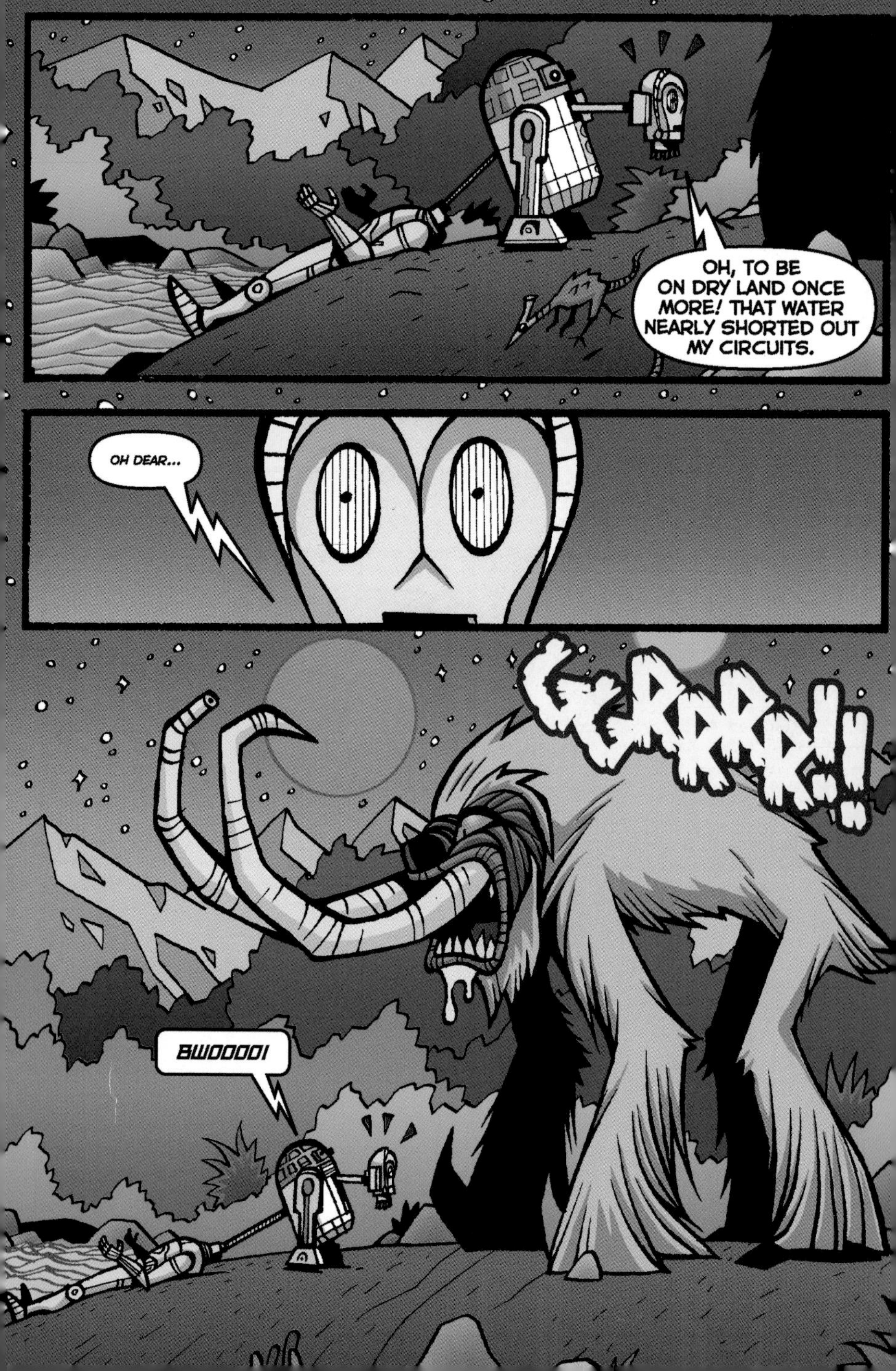
OH, TO BE ON DRY LAND ONCE MORE! THAT WATER NEARLY SHORTED OUT MY CIRCUITS.
OH DEAR...
GRRRR!!!
BWOOOOI

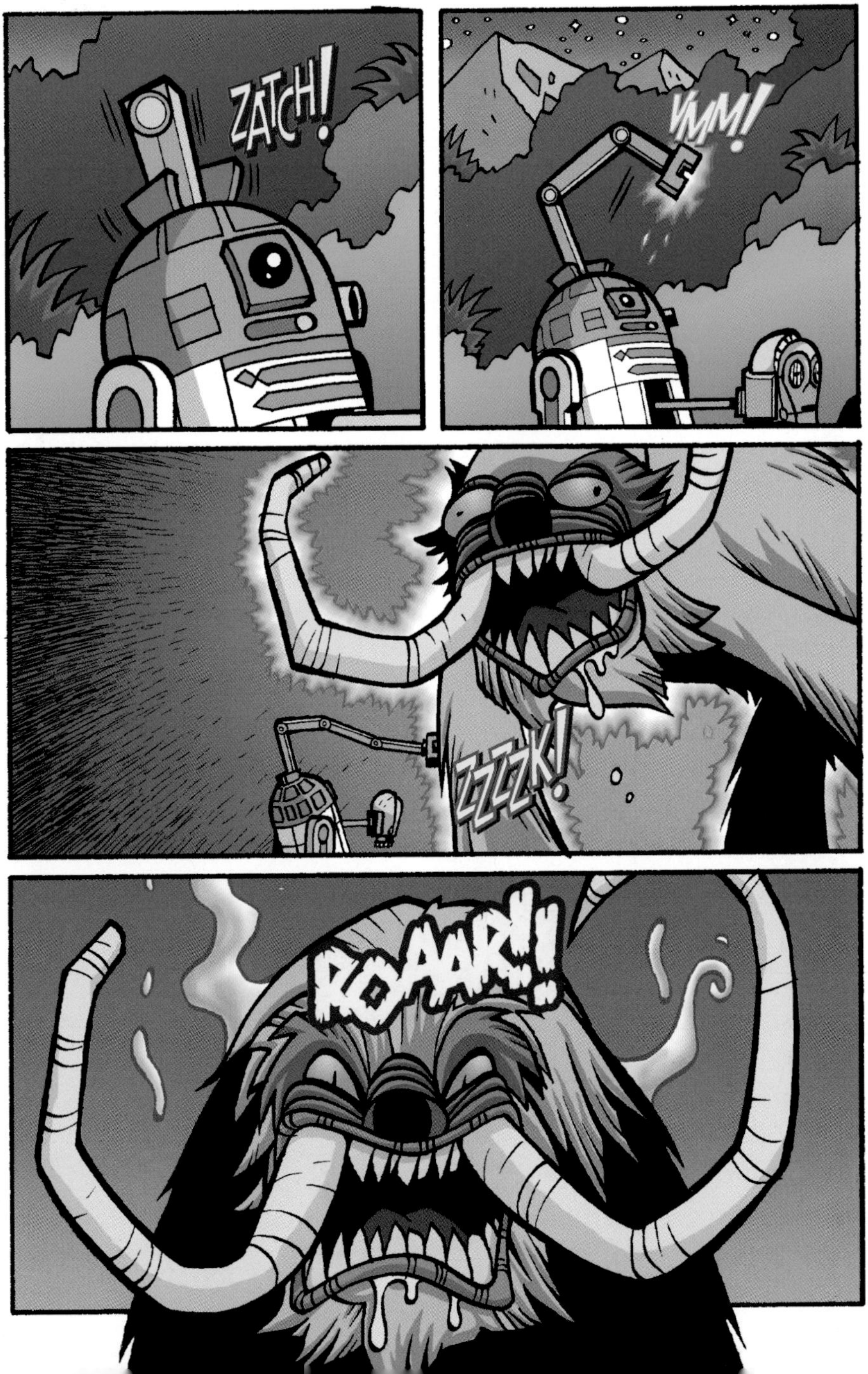
ZATCH!
VMM!
ZZZZK!
ROAAR!!

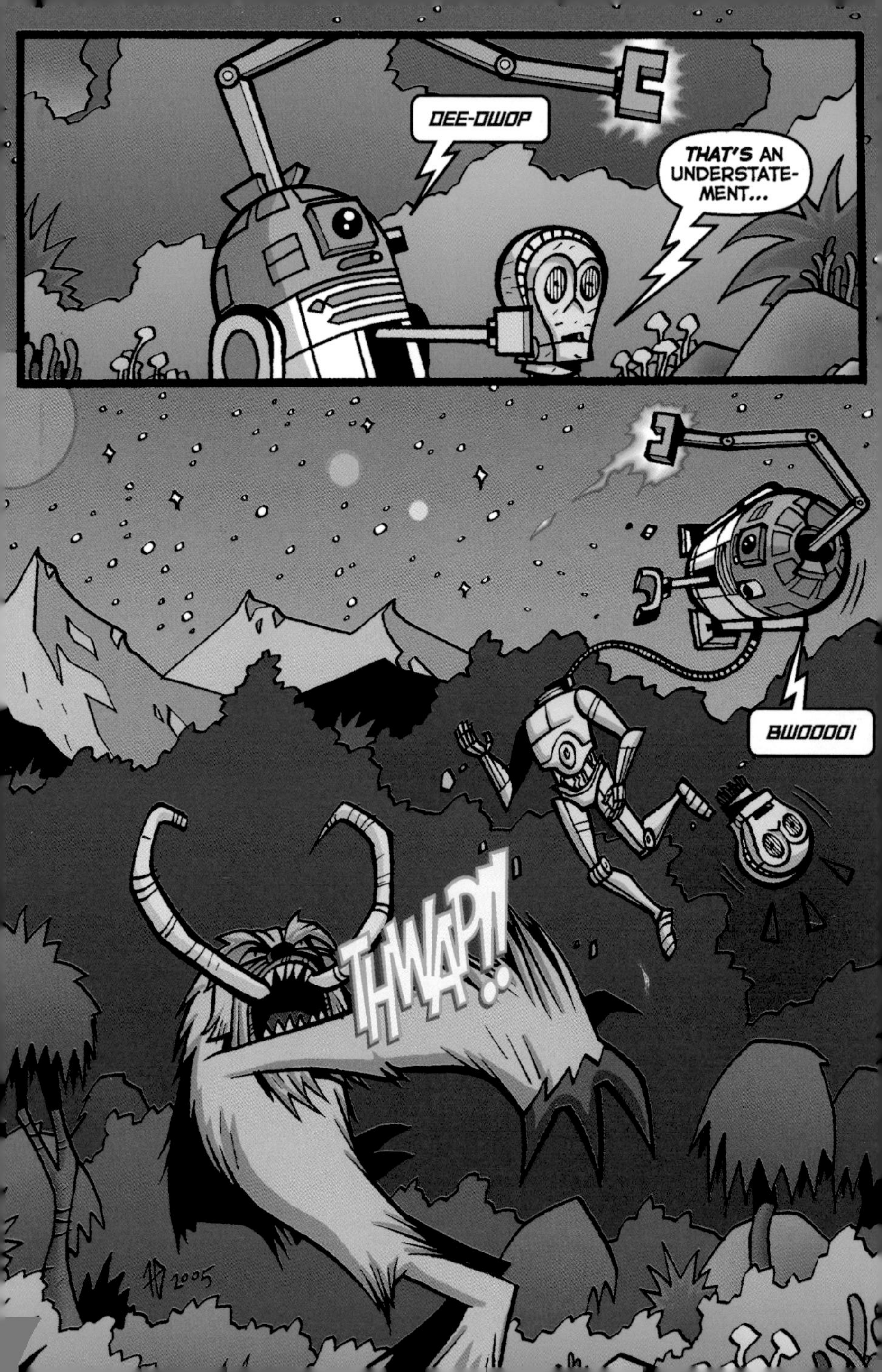
DEE-DWOP
THAT'S AN UNDERSTATE-MENT...
BWOOOO!
THWAP!!

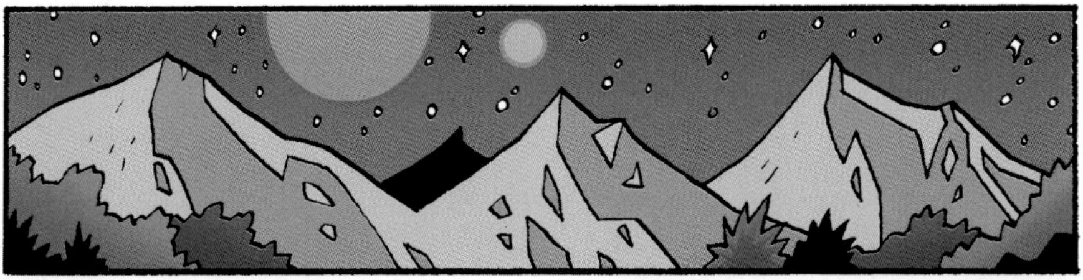

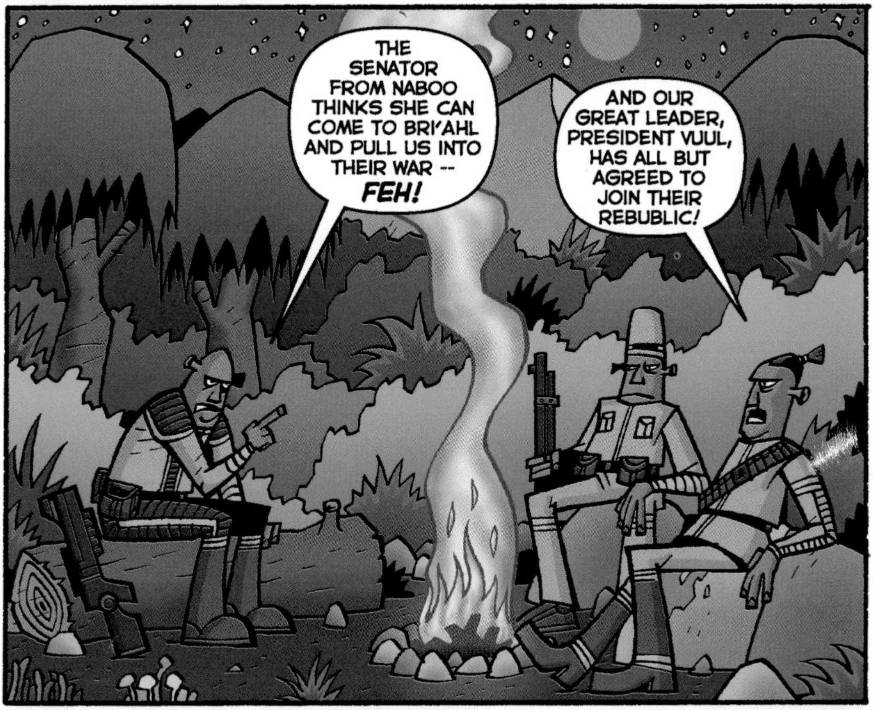
THE SENATOR FROM NABOO THINKS SHE CAN COME TO BRI'AHL AND PULL US INTO THEIR WAR -- FEH!
AND OUR GREAT LEADER, PRESIDENT VUUL, HAS ALL BUT AGREED TO JOIN THEIR REBUBLIC!

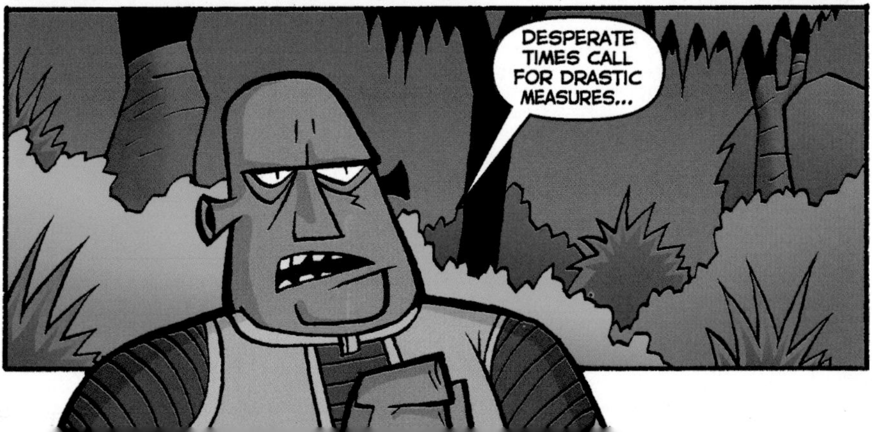
DESPERATE TIMES CALL FOR DRASTIC MEASURES...

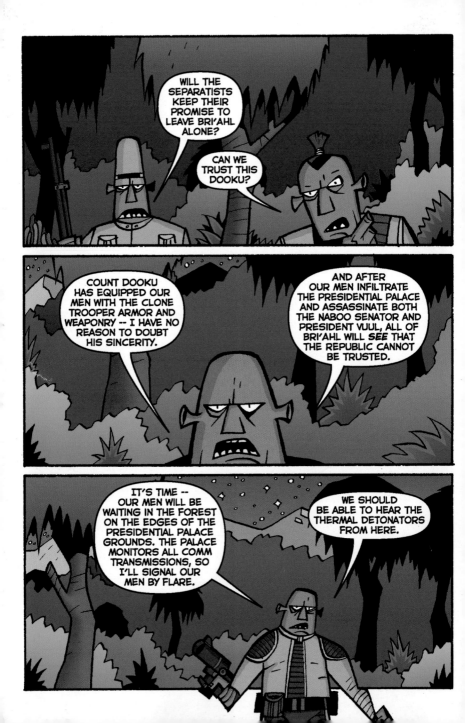

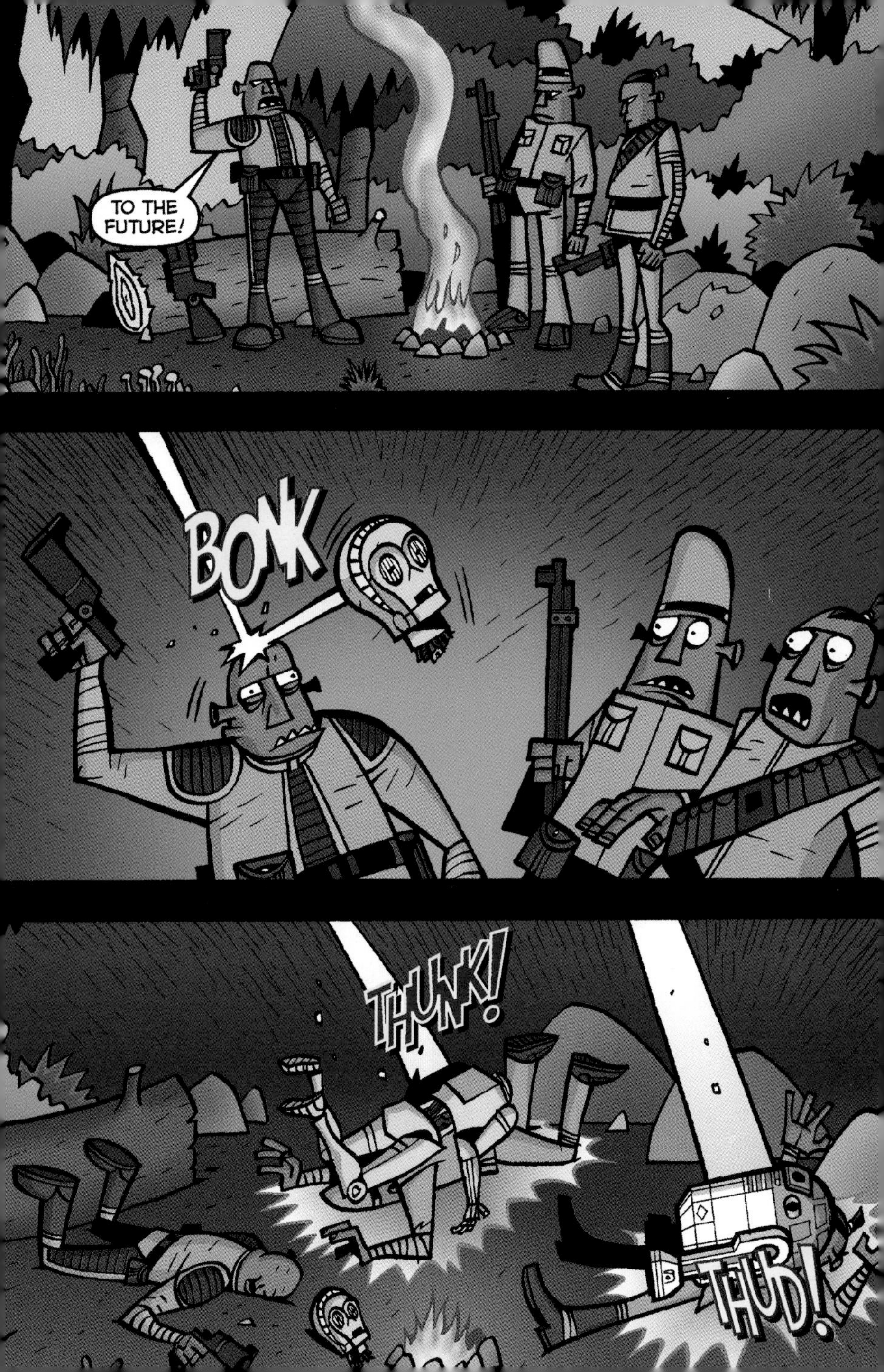
TO THE FUTURE!
BONK
THUNK!
THUD!

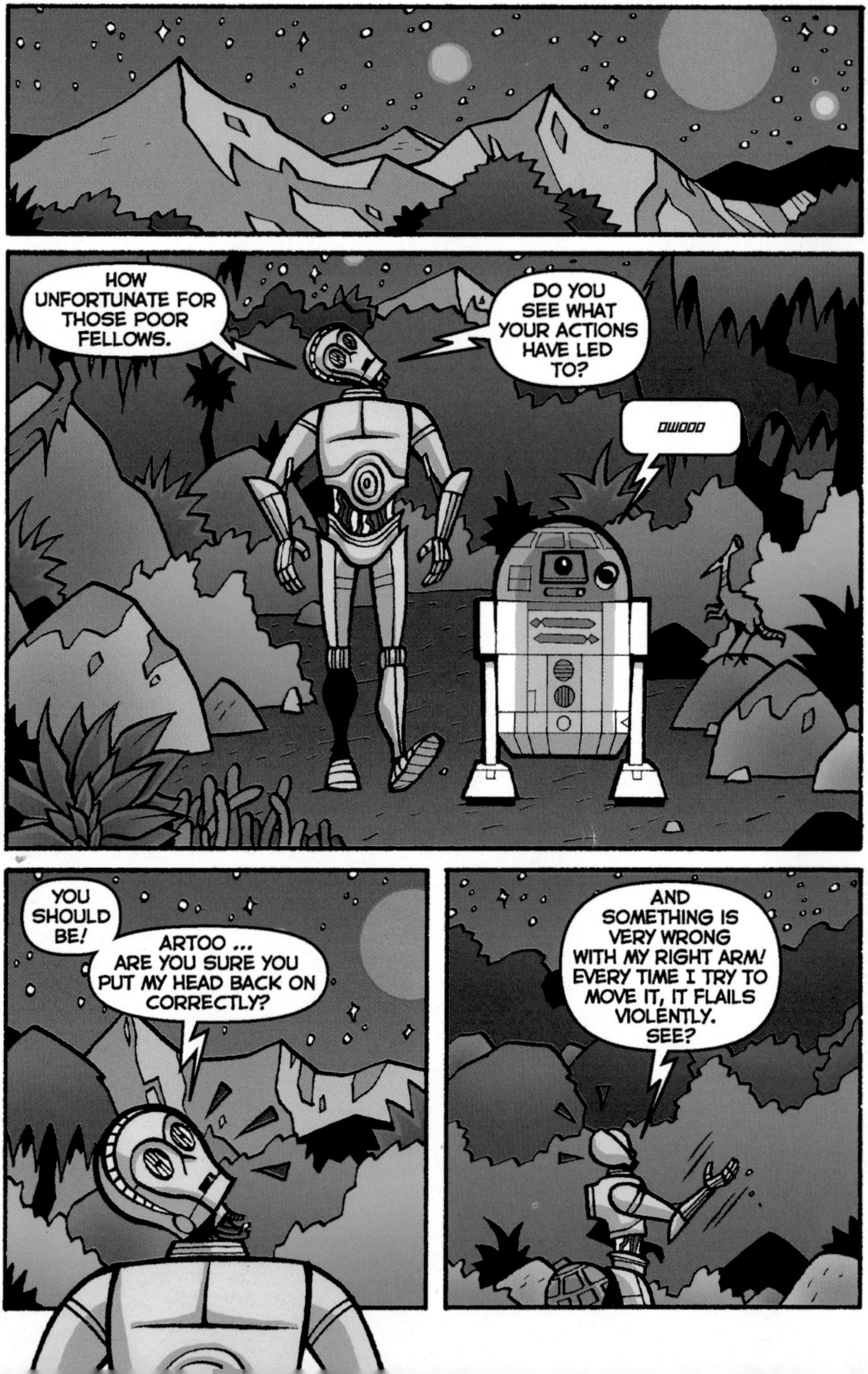
HOW UNFORTUNATE FOR THOSE POOR FELLOWS.
DO YOU SEE WHAT YOUR ACTIONS HAVE LED TO?
OWOOO
YOU SHOULD BE!
ARTOO ... ARE YOU SURE YOU PUT MY HEAD BACK ON CORRECTLY?
AND SOMETHING IS VERY WRONG WITH MY RIGHT ARM! EVERY TIME I TRY TO MOVE IT, IT FLAILS VIOLENTLY. SEE?

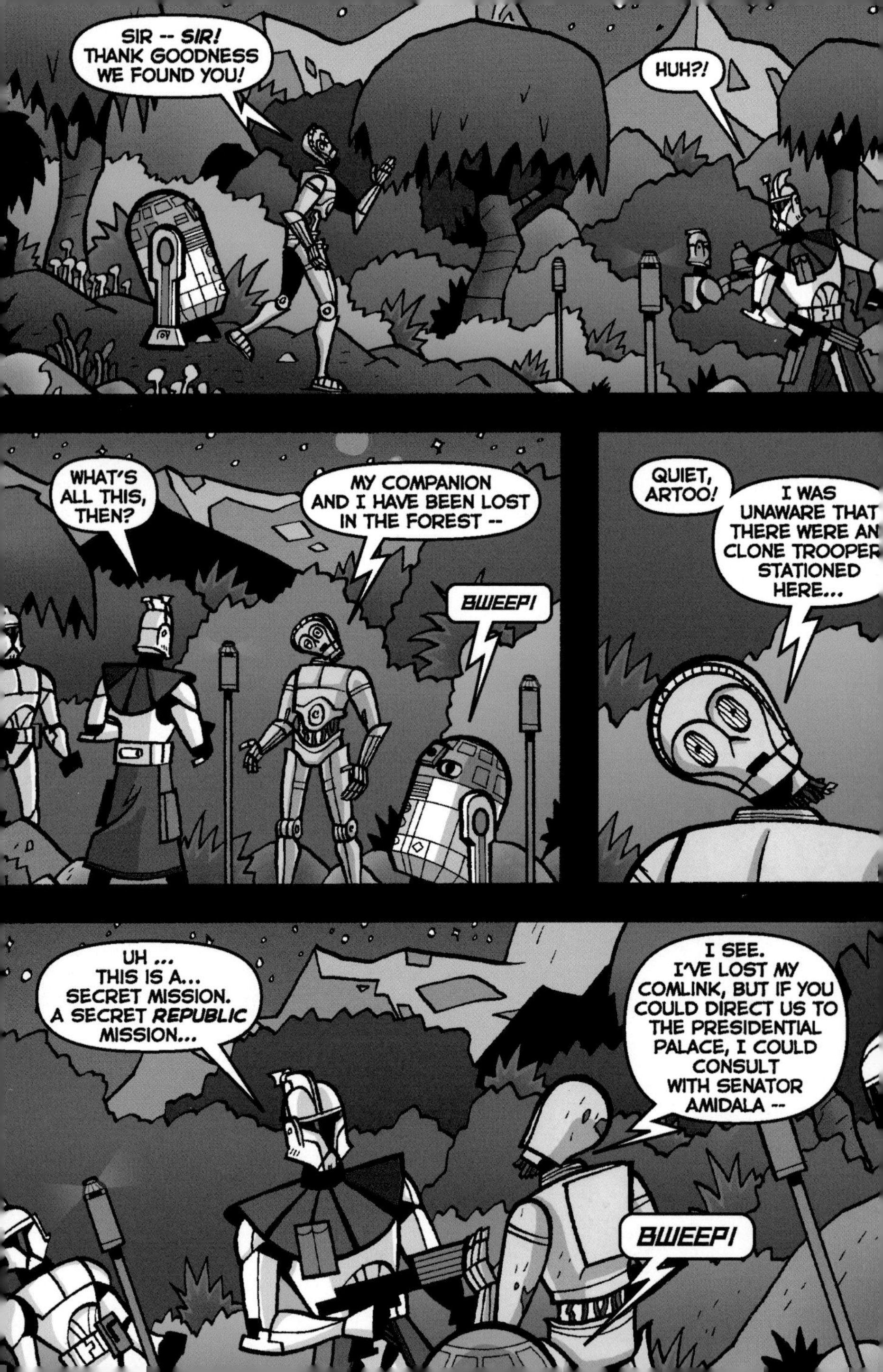
SIR -- SIR! THANK GOODNESS WE FOUND YOU!
HUH?!
WHAT'S ALL THIS, THEN?
MY COMPANION AND I HAVE BEEN LOST IN THE FOREST --
BWEEP!
QUIET, ARTOO!
I WAS UNAWARE THAT THERE WERE AN CLONE TROOPER STATIONED HERE...
UH ... THIS IS A... SECRET MISSION. A SECRET REPUBLIC MISSION...
I SEE. I'VE LOST MY COMLINK, BUT IF YOU COULD DIRECT US TO THE PRESIDENTIAL PALACE, I COULD CONSULT WITH SENATOR AMIDALA --
BWEEP!

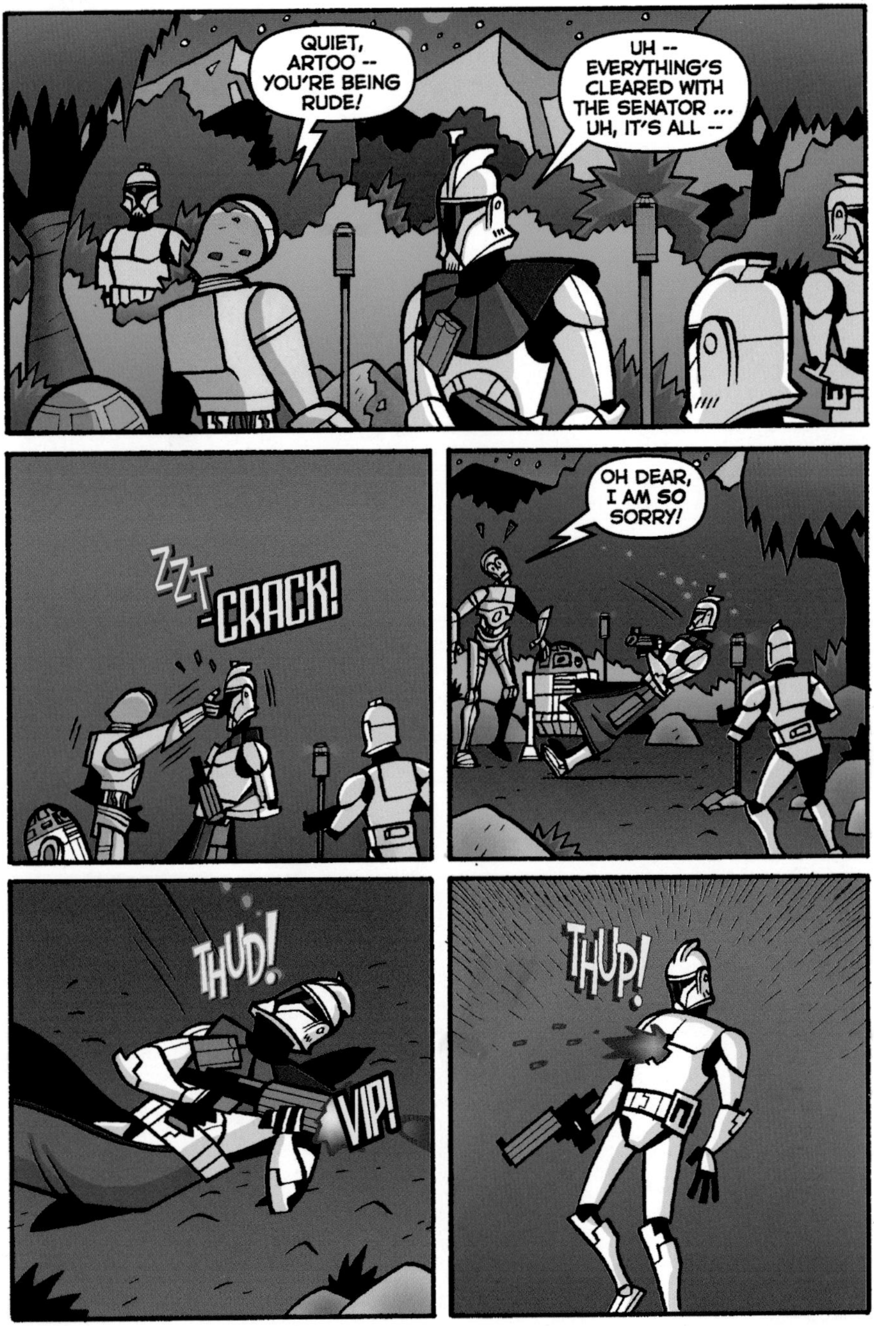
QUIET, ARTOO -- YOU'RE BEING RUDE!
UH -- EVERYTHING'S CLEARED WITH THE SENATOR ... UH, IT'S ALL --
ZZT-CRACK!
OH DEAR, I AM SO SORRY!
THUD!
VIP!
THUP!

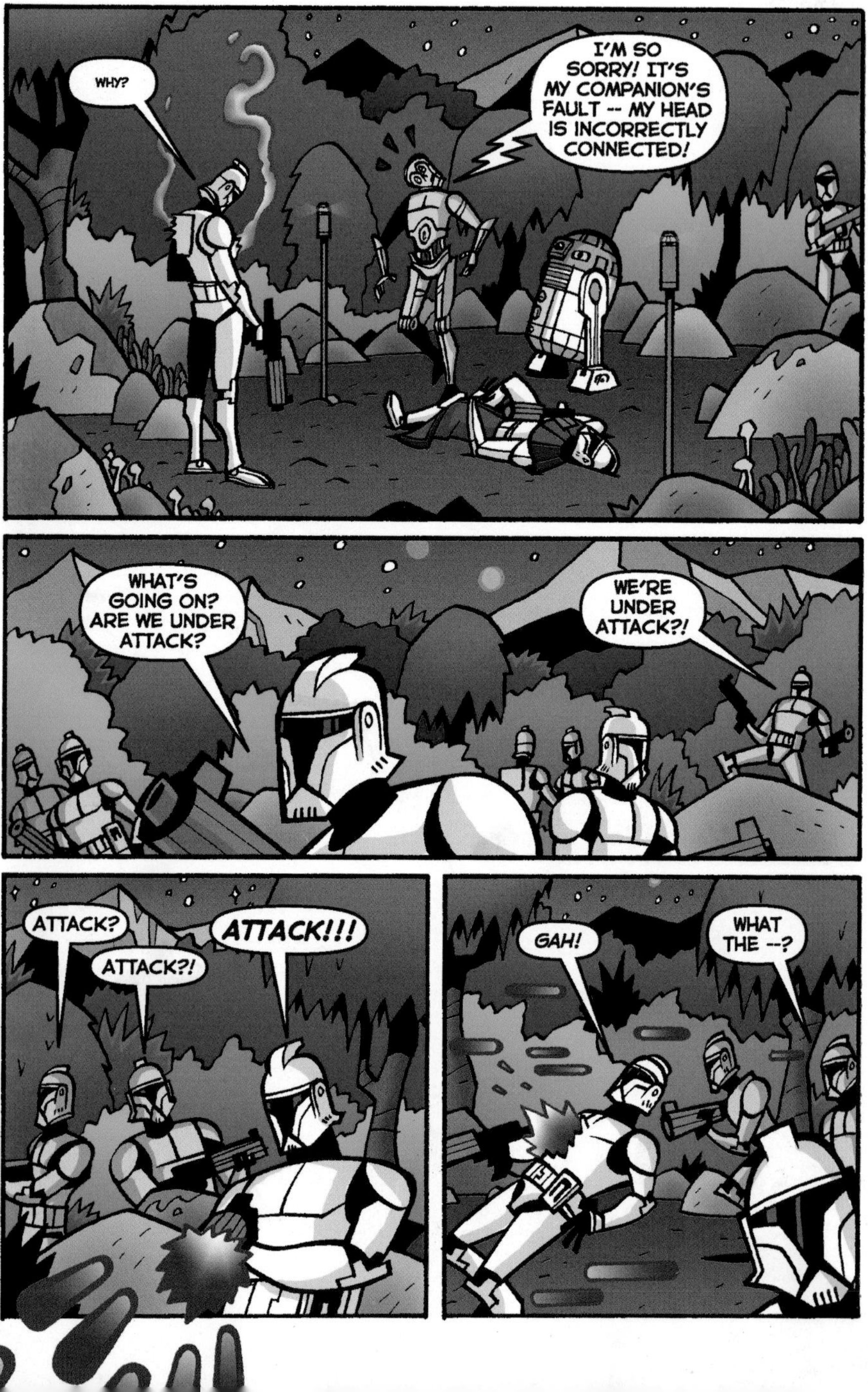
WHY?
I'M SO SORRY! IT'S MY COMPANION'S FAULT -- MY HEAD IS INCORRECTLY CONNECTED!
WHAT'S GOING ON? ARE WE UNDER ATTACK?
WE'RE UNDER ATTACK?!
ATTACK?
ATTACK?!
ATTACK!!!
GAH!
WHAT THE --?

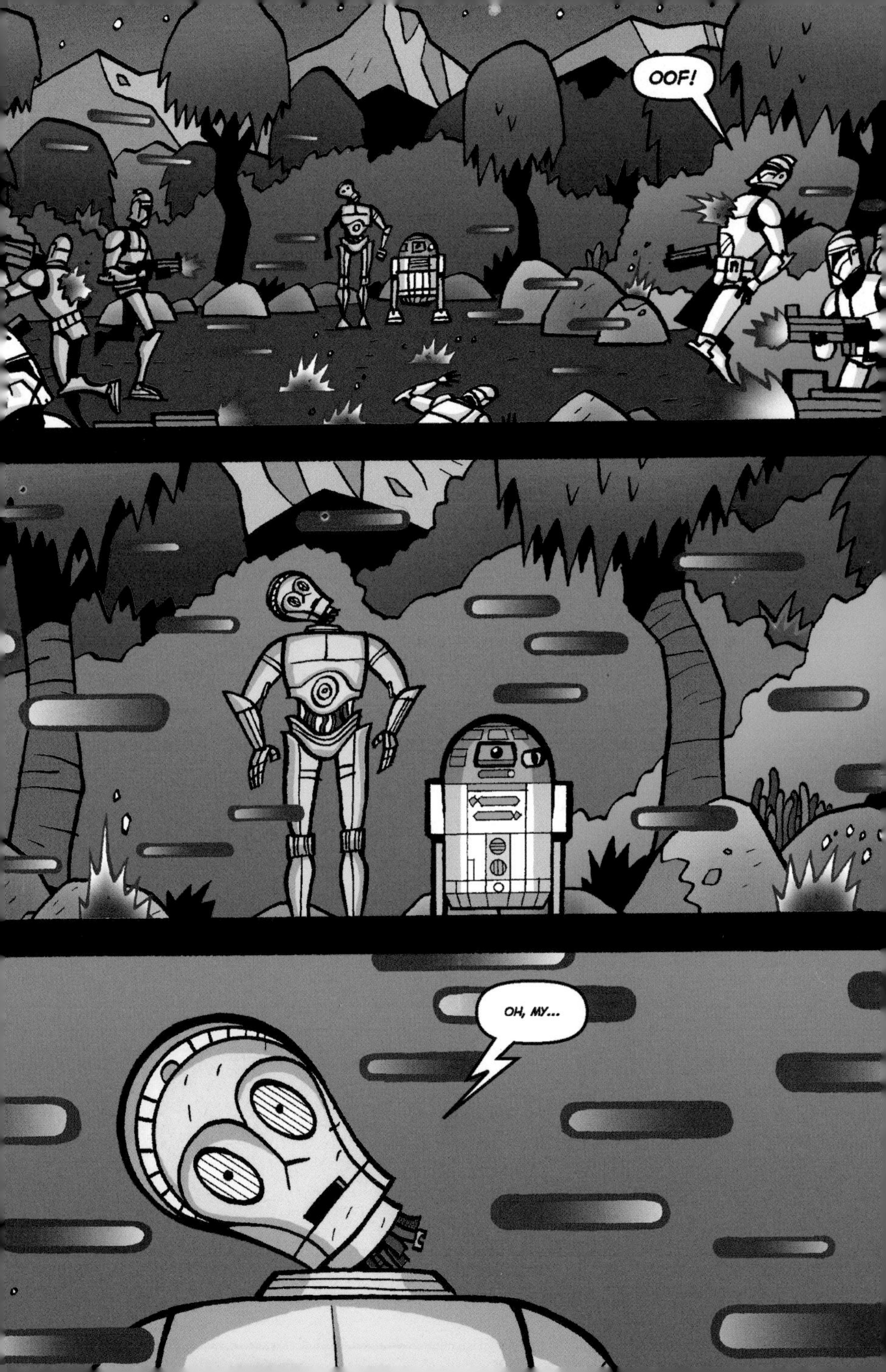
OOF!
OH, MY...

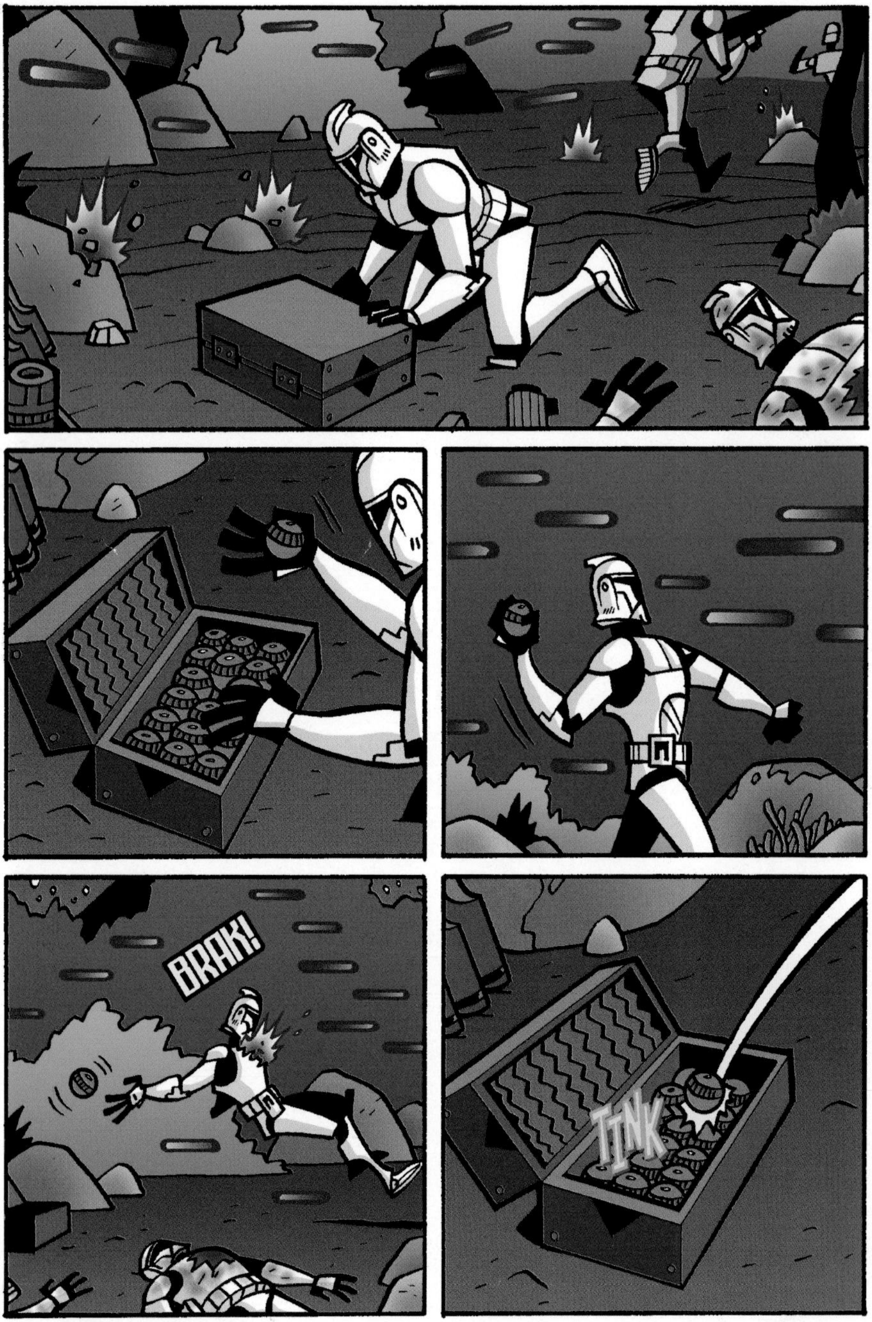
BRAK!
TINK

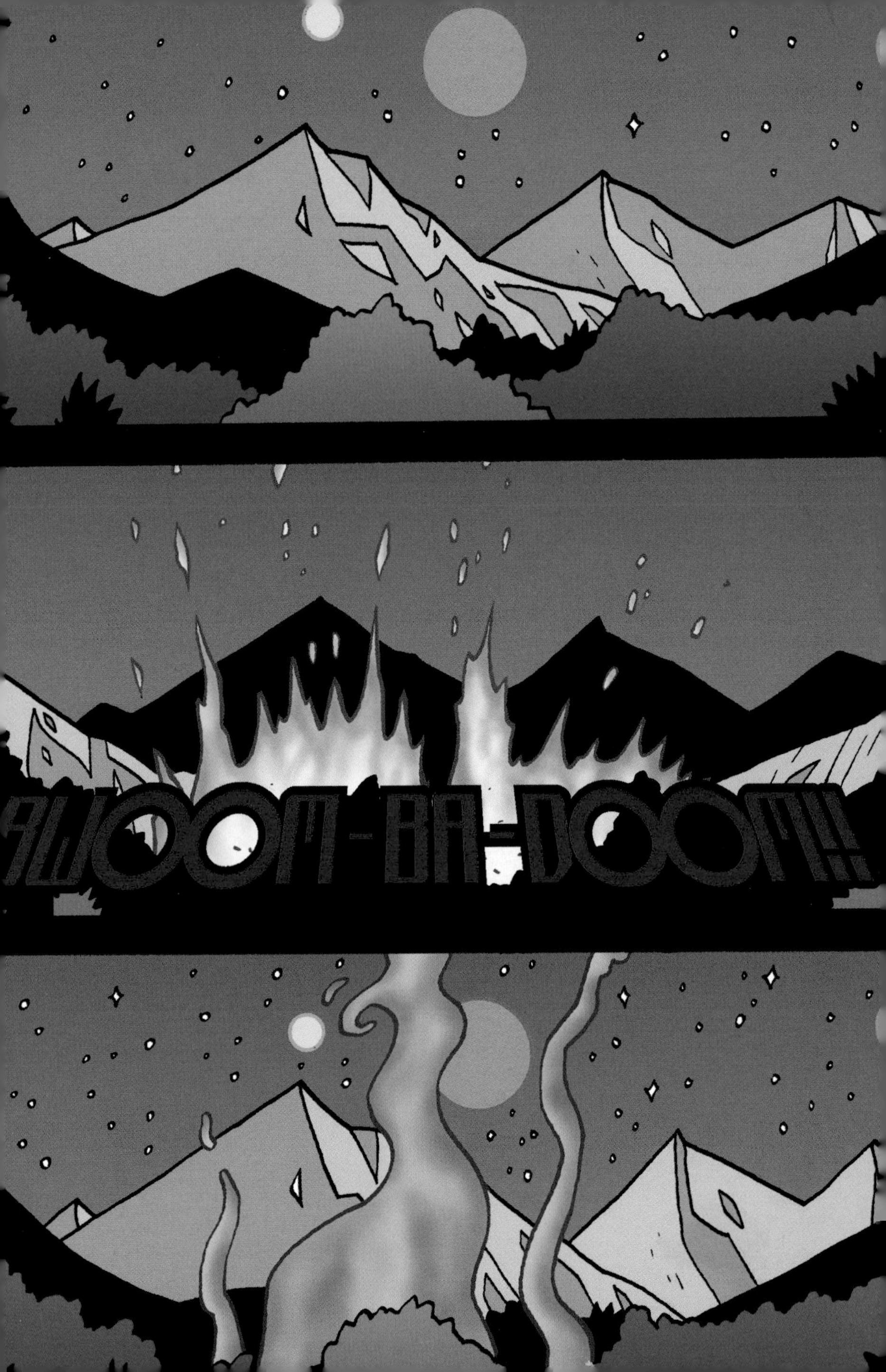
SWOOM-BA-DOOM!!

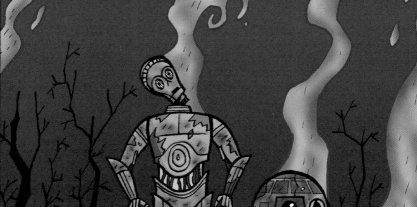

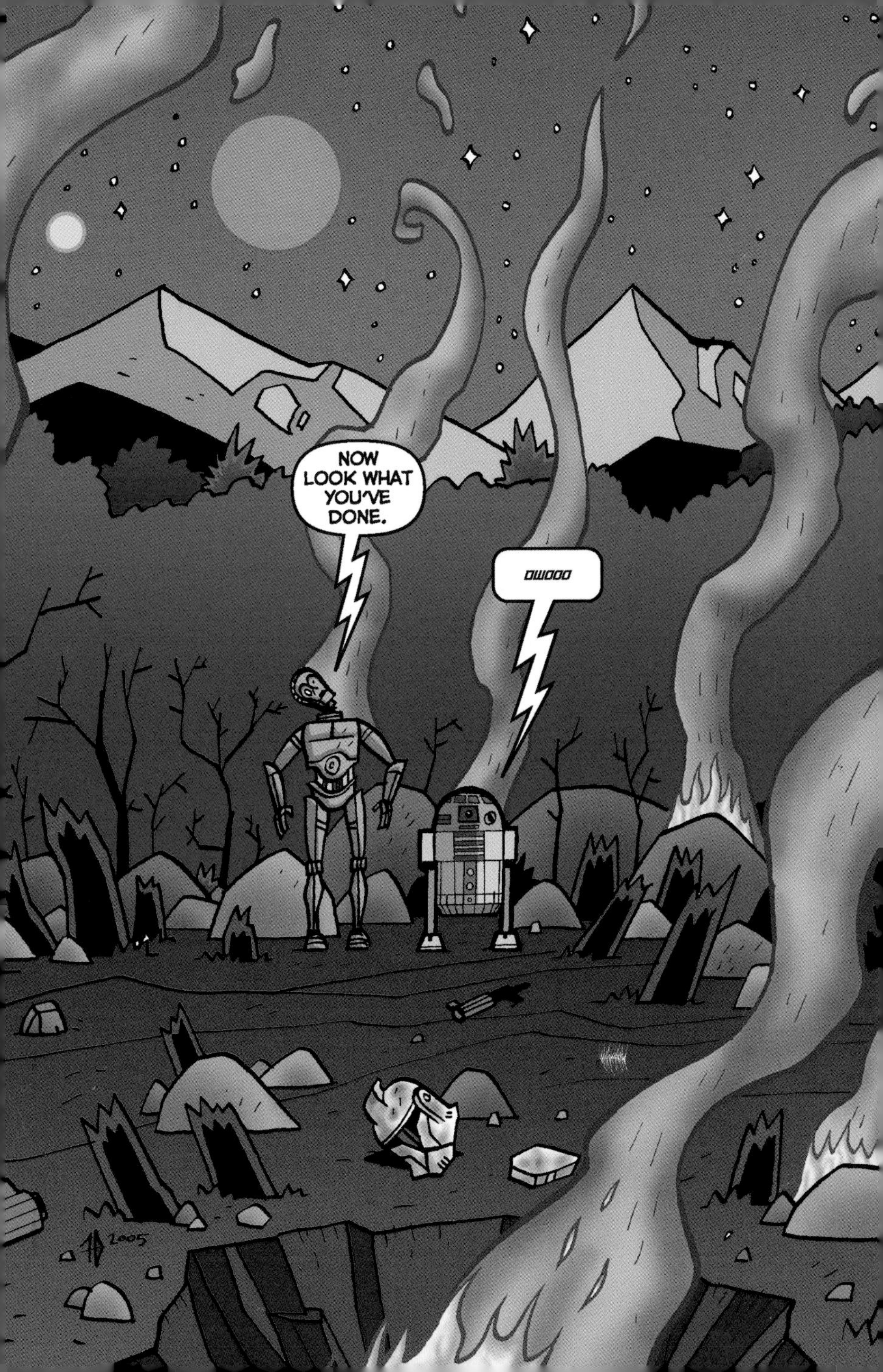
NOW LOOK WHAT YOU'VE DONE.
DWOOO
2005

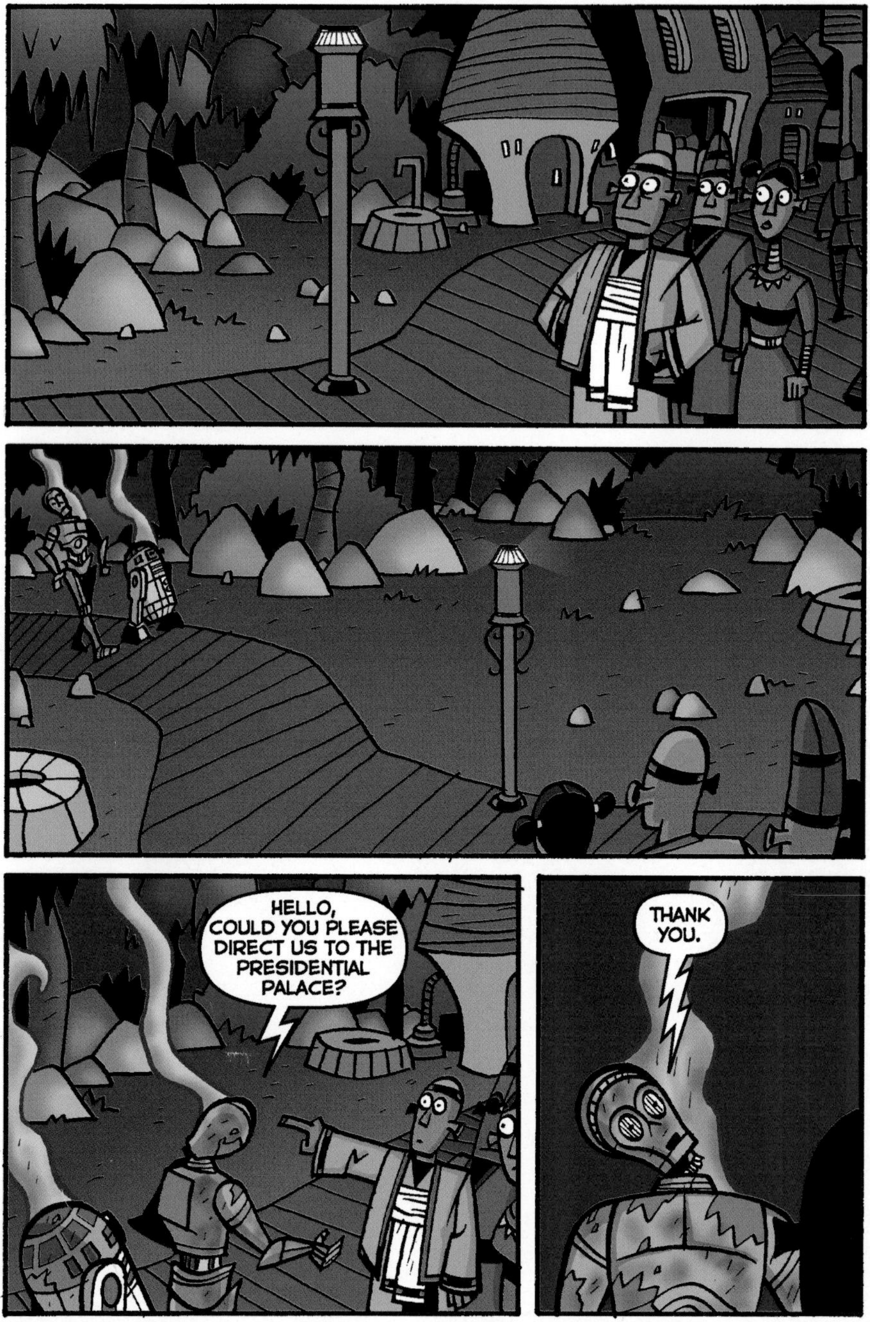
HELLO, COULD YOU PLEASE DIRECT US TO THE PRESIDENTIAL PALACE?
THANK YOU.

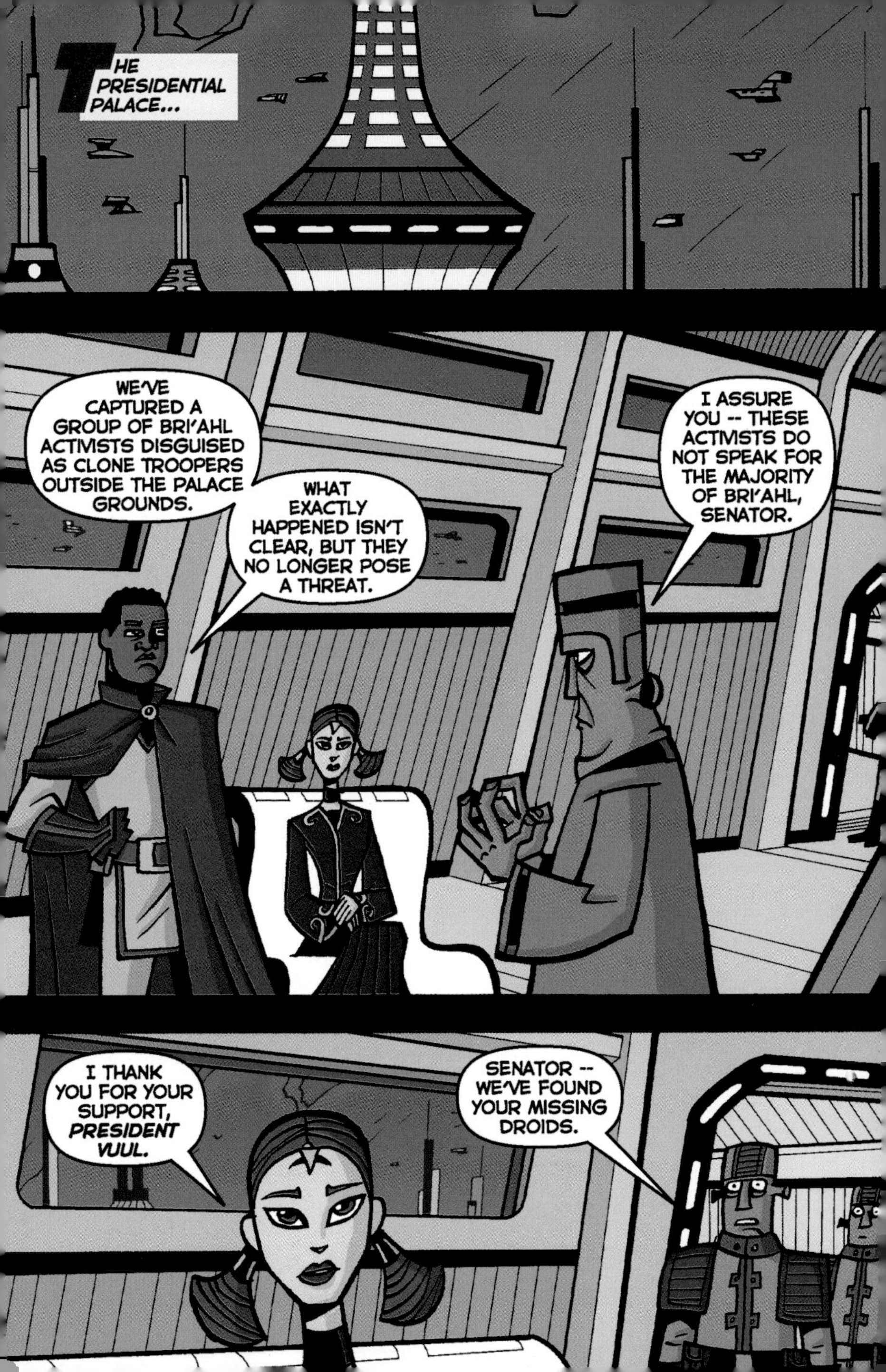
THE PRESIDENTIAL PALACE...
WE'VE CAPTURED A GROUP OF BRI'AHL ACTIVISTS DISGUISED AS CLONE TROOPERS OUTSIDE THE PALACE GROUNDS.
WHAT EXACTLY HAPPENED ISN'T CLEAR, BUT THEY NO LONGER POSE A THREAT.
I ASSURE YOU -- THESE ACTIVISTS DO NOT SPEAK FOR THE MAJORITY OF BRI'AHL, SENATOR.
I THANK YOU FOR YOUR SUPPORT, *PRESIDENT VUUL.*
SENATOR -- WE'VE FOUND YOUR MISSING DROIDS.

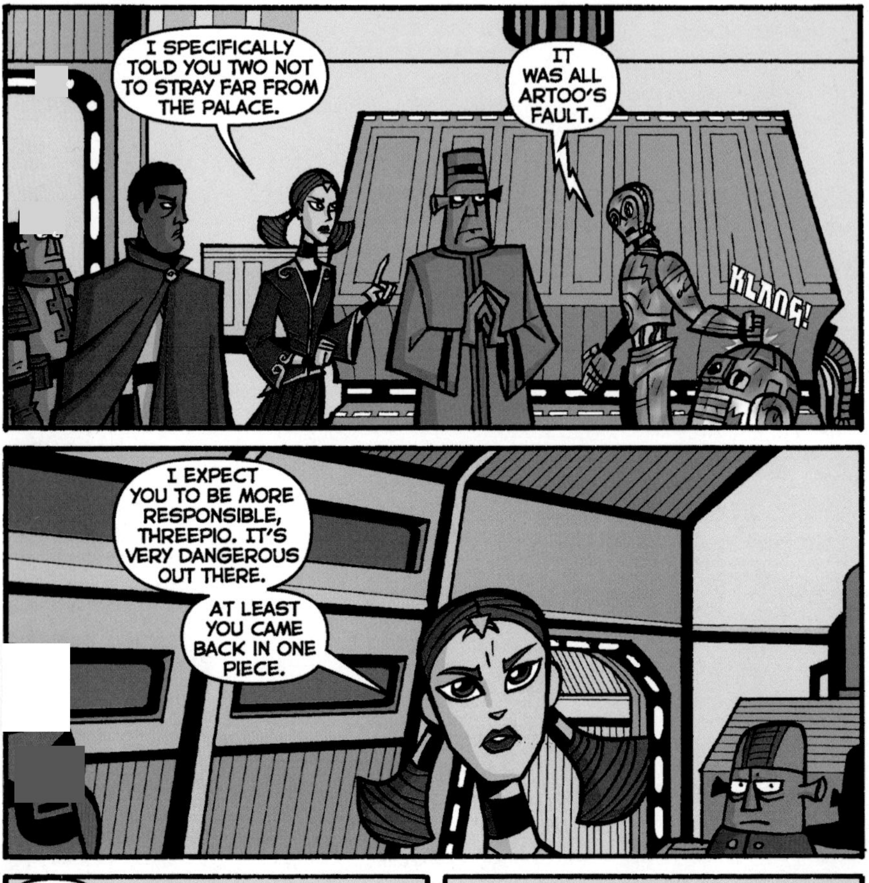
I SPECIFICALLY TOLD YOU TWO NOT TO STRAY FAR FROM THE PALACE.
IT WAS ALL ARTOO'S FAULT.
KLANG!
I EXPECT YOU TO BE MORE RESPONSIBLE, THREEPIO. IT'S VERY DANGEROUS OUT THERE.
AT LEAST YOU CAME BACK IN ONE PIECE.
...
CLANK!
THE END

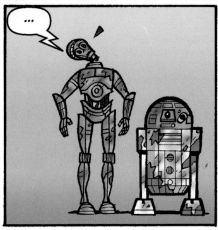

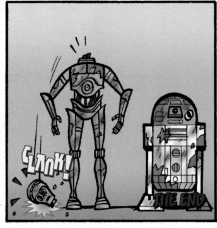

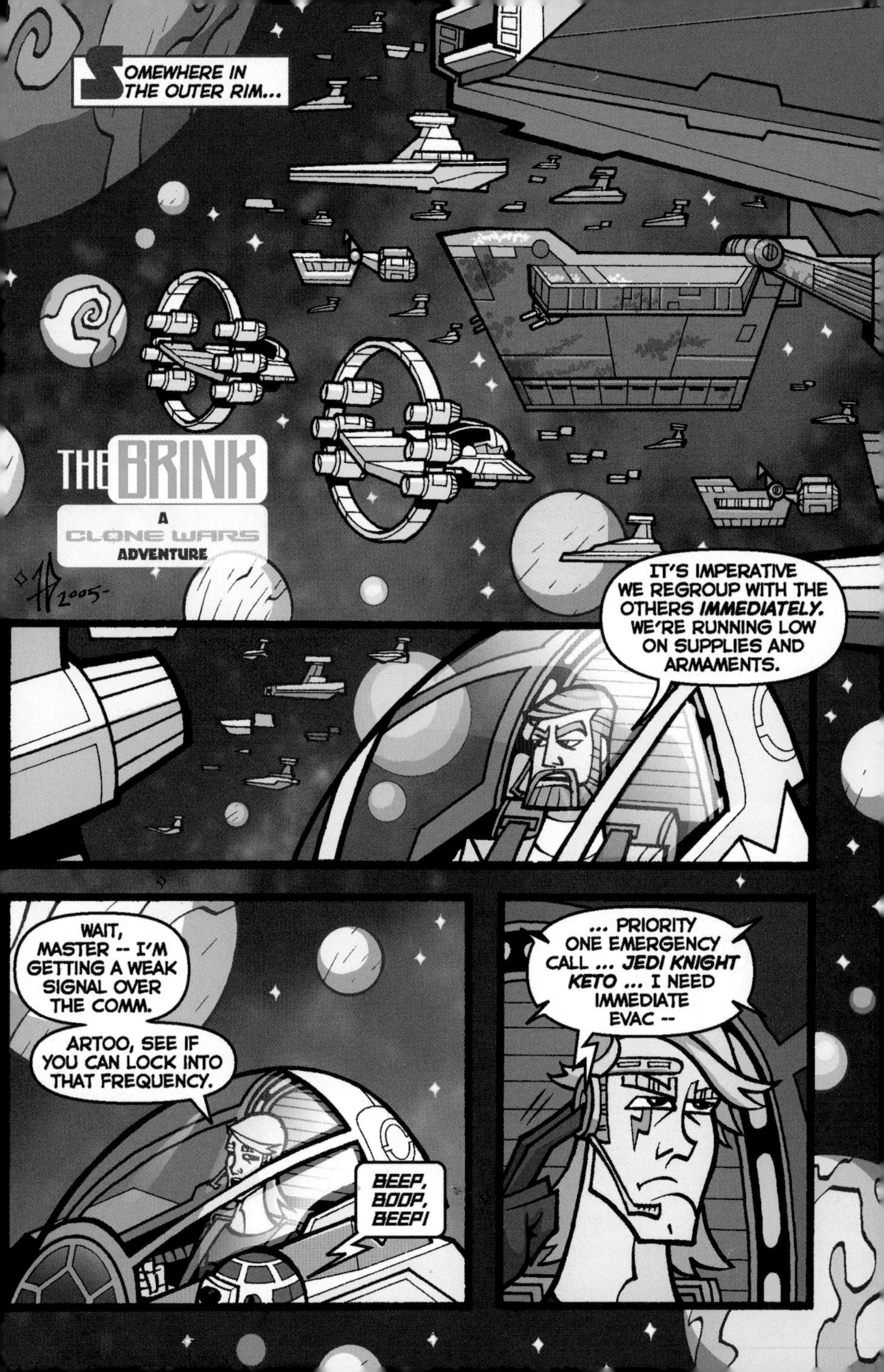
SOMEWHERE IN THE OUTER RIM...
THE BRINK
A CLONE WARS ADVENTURE
IT'S IMPERATIVE WE REGROUP WITH THE OTHERS IMMEDIATELY. WE'RE RUNNING LOW ON SUPPLIES AND ARMAMENTS.
WAIT, MASTER -- I'M GETTING A WEAK SIGNAL OVER THE COMM.
ARTOO, SEE IF YOU CAN LOCK INTO THAT FREQUENCY.
BEEP, BOOP, BEEP!
... PRIORITY ONE EMERGENCY CALL ... JEDI KNIGHT KETO ... I NEED IMMEDIATE EVAC --

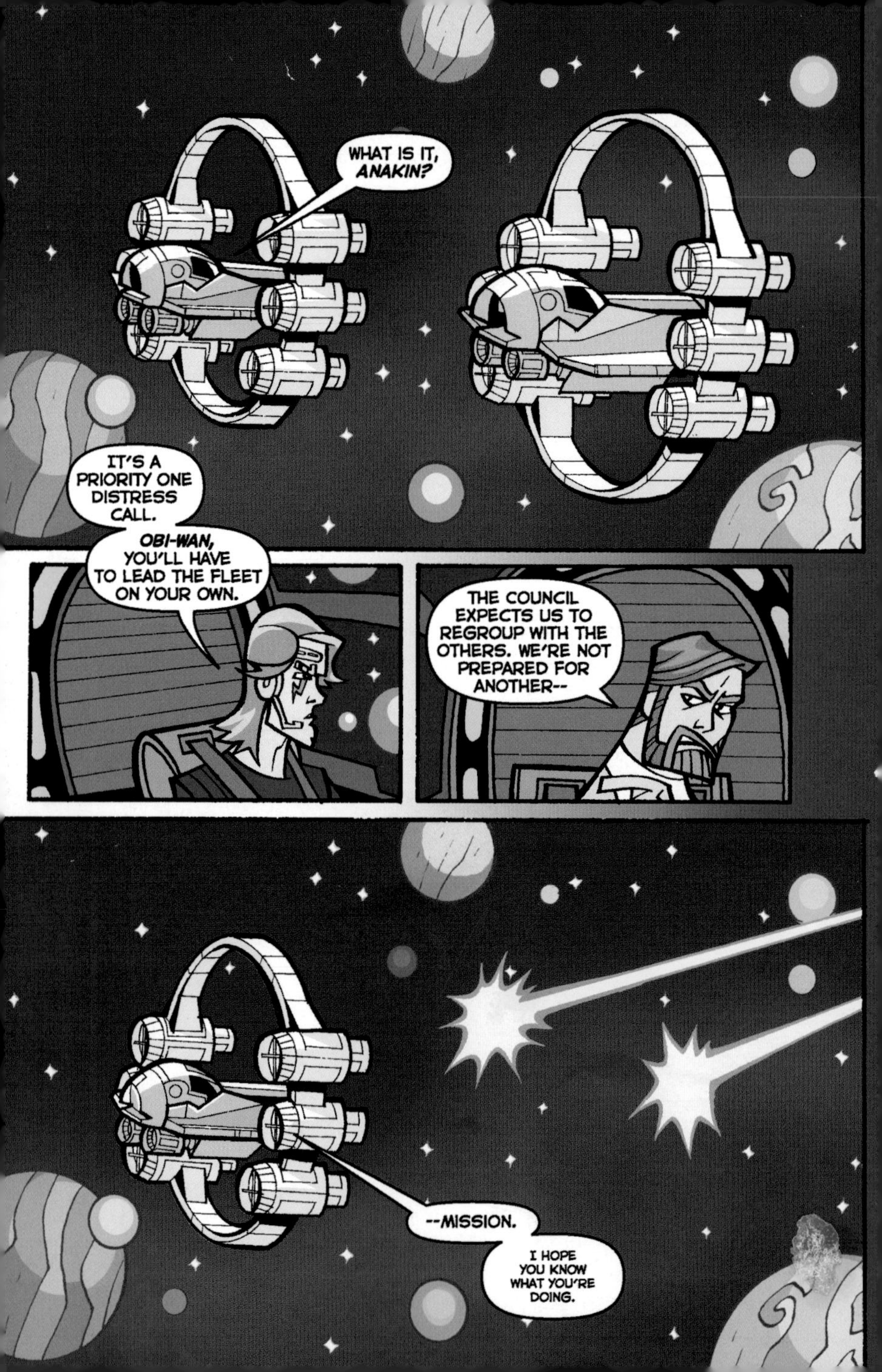
WHAT IS IT, ANAKIN?
IT'S A PRIORITY ONE DISTRESS CALL.
OBI-WAN, YOU'LL HAVE TO LEAD THE FLEET ON YOUR OWN.
THE COUNCIL EXPECTS US TO REGROUP WITH THE OTHERS. WE'RE NOT PREPARED FOR ANOTHER--
--MISSION.
I HOPE YOU KNOW WHAT YOU'RE DOING.

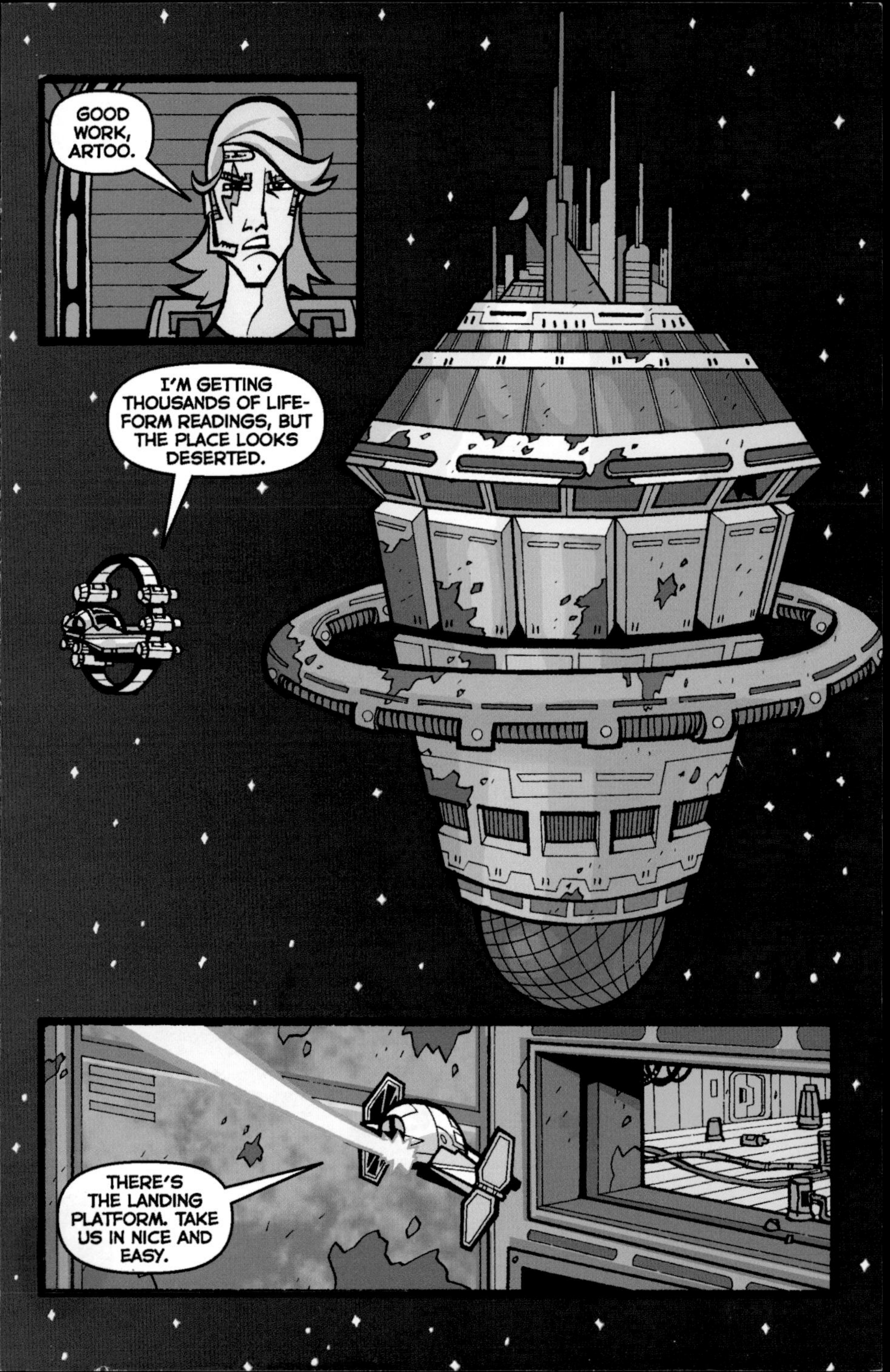
GOOD WORK, ARTOO.
I'M GETTING THOUSANDS OF LIFE-FORM READINGS, BUT THE PLACE LOOKS DESERTED.
THERE'S THE LANDING PLATFORM. TAKE US IN NICE AND EASY.

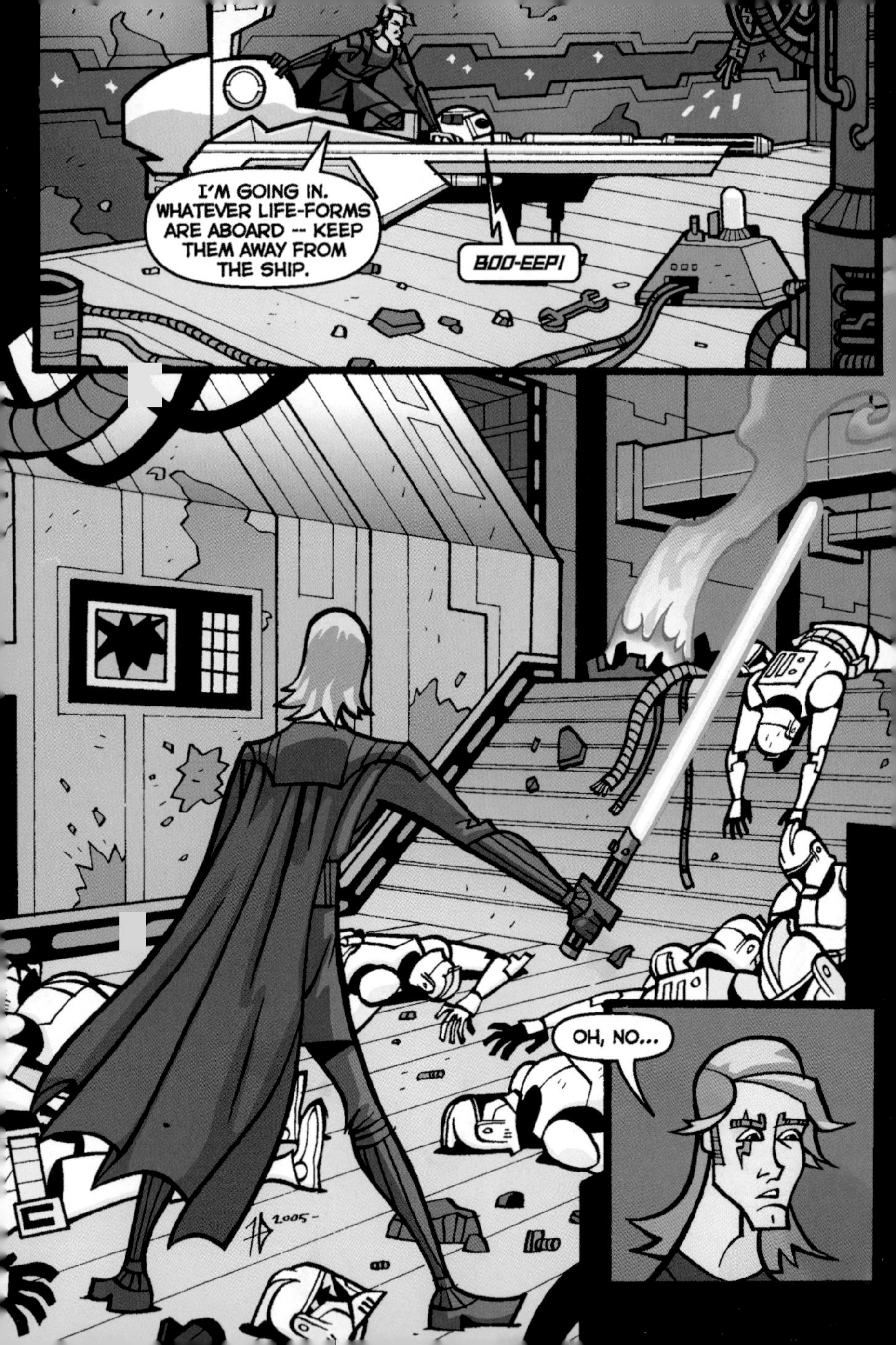
I'M GOING IN. WHATEVER LIFE-FORMS ARE ABOARD -- KEEP THEM AWAY FROM THE SHIP.
BOO-EEP!
OH, NO...

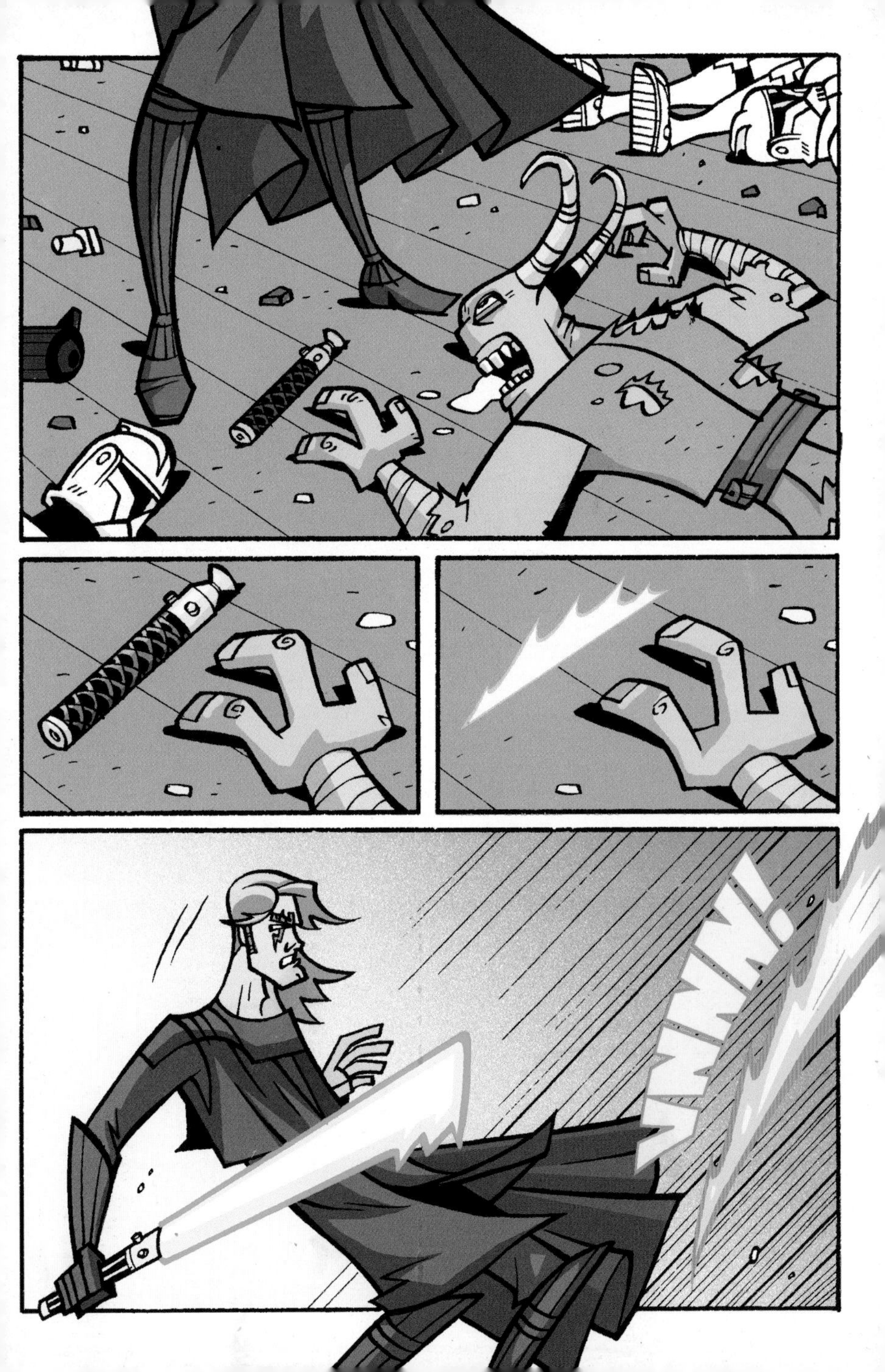
VMMM!

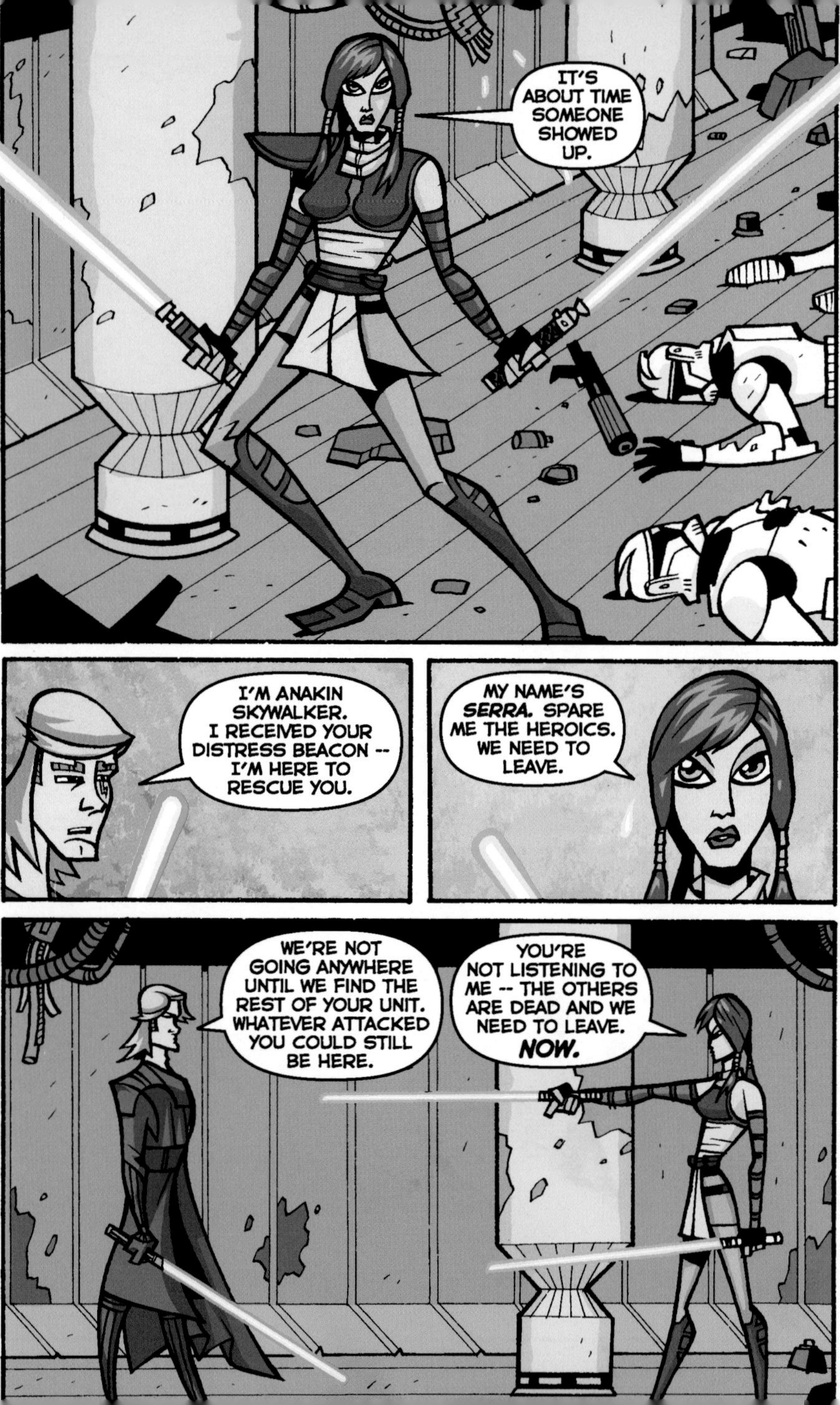
IT'S ABOUT TIME SOMEONE SHOWED UP.
I'M ANAKIN SKYWALKER. I RECEIVED YOUR DISTRESS BEACON -- I'M HERE TO RESCUE YOU.
MY NAME'S *SERRA.* SPARE ME THE HEROICS. WE NEED TO LEAVE.
WE'RE NOT GOING ANYWHERE UNTIL WE FIND THE REST OF YOUR UNIT. WHATEVER ATTACKED YOU COULD STILL BE HERE.
YOU'RE NOT LISTENING TO ME -- THE OTHERS ARE DEAD AND WE NEED TO LEAVE. ***NOW.***

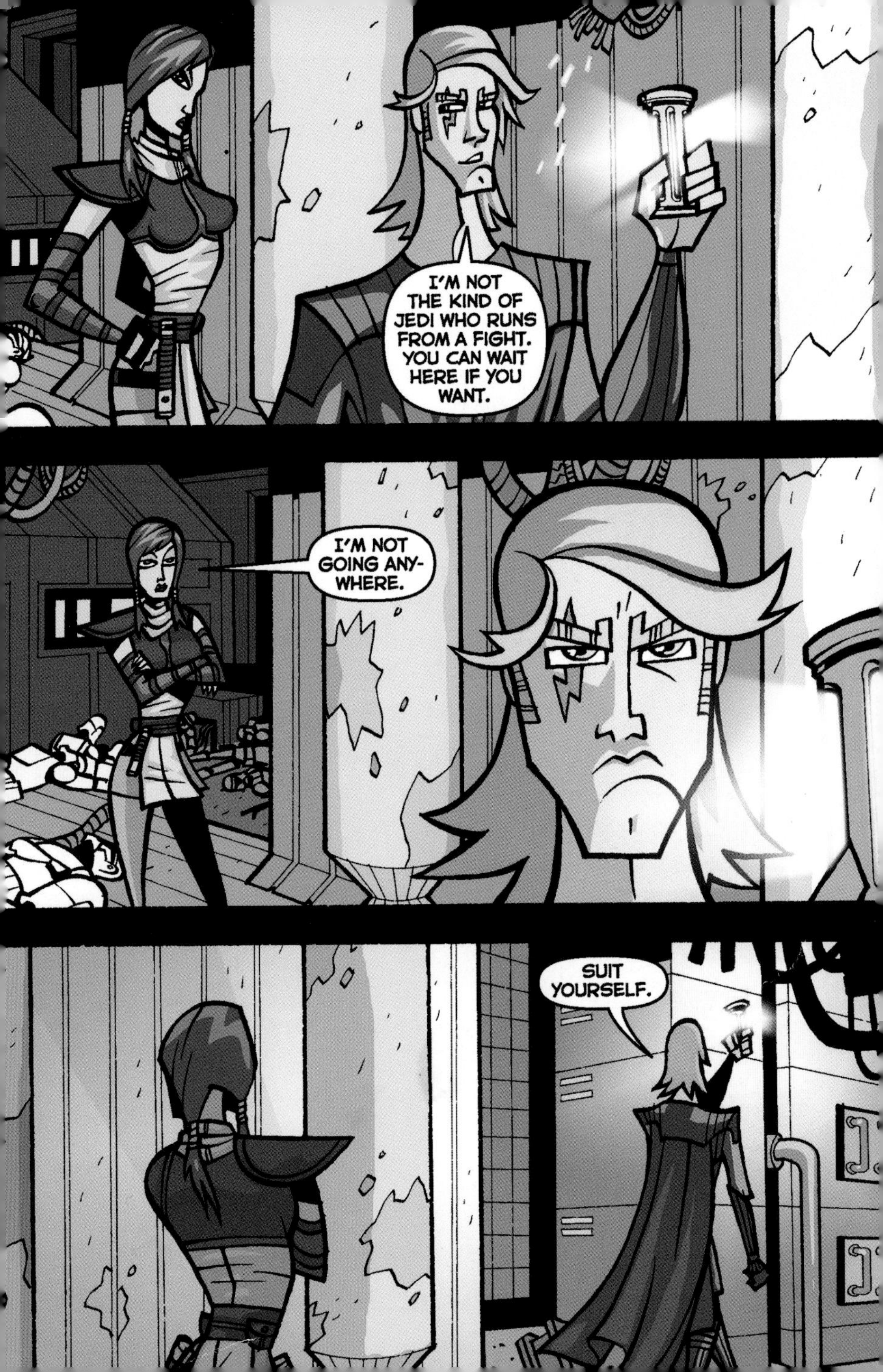
I'M NOT THE KIND OF JEDI WHO RUNS FROM A FIGHT. YOU CAN WAIT HERE IF YOU WANT.
I'M NOT GOING ANY-WHERE.
SUIT YOURSELF.

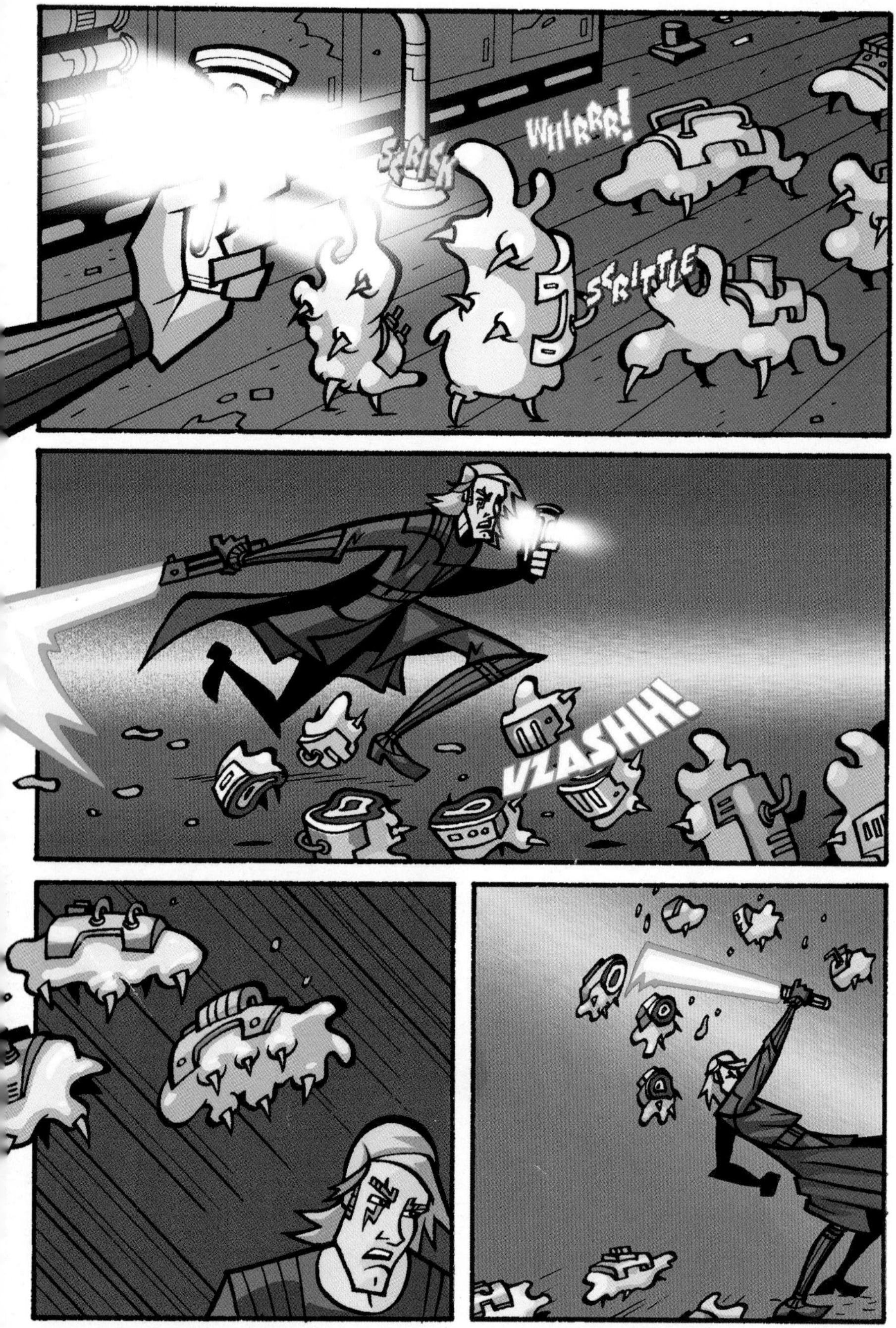

WHIRRR!
SCRISK
SCRITTLE
VZASHH!

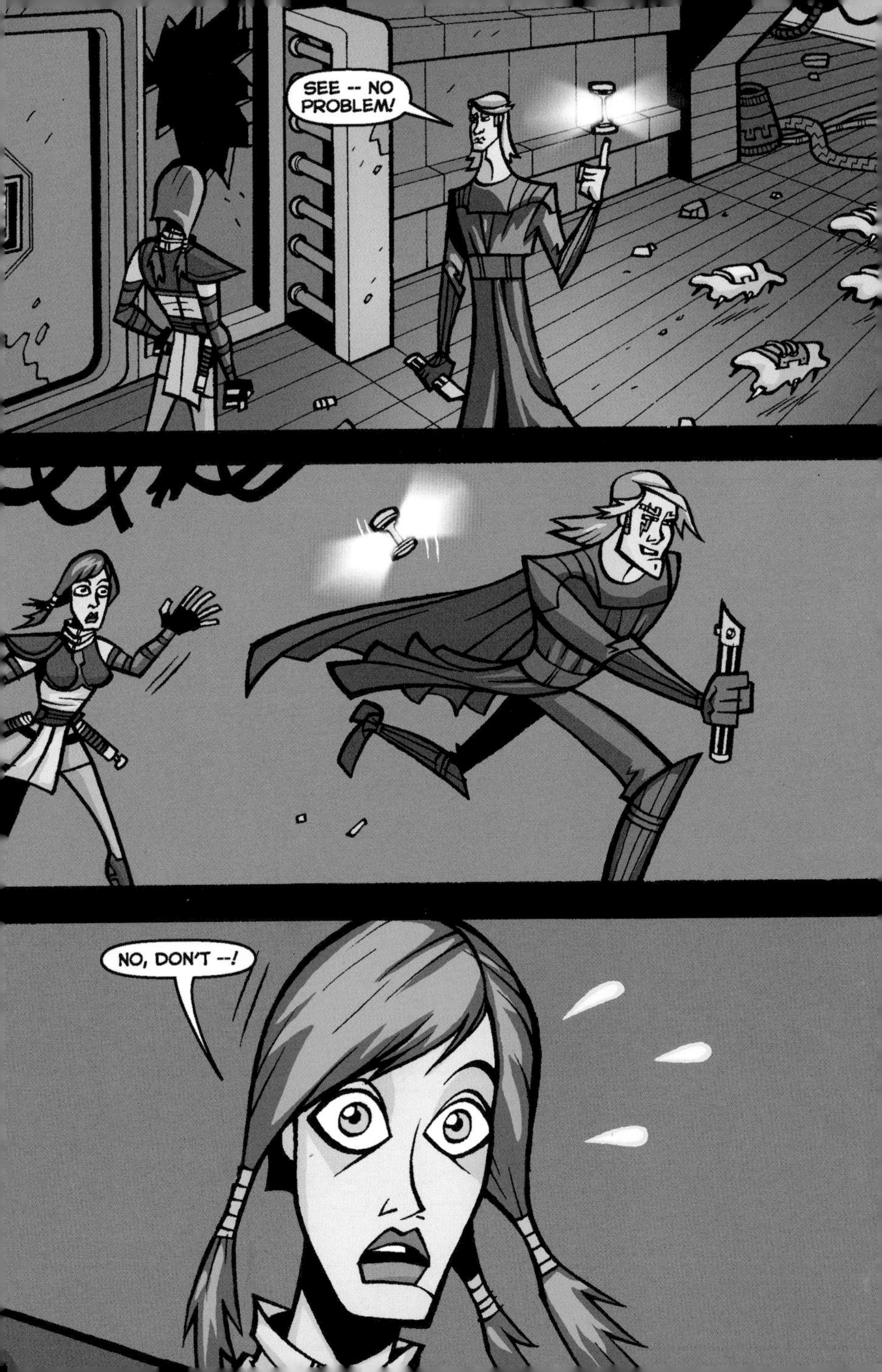
SEE -- NO PROBLEM!
NO, DON'T --!

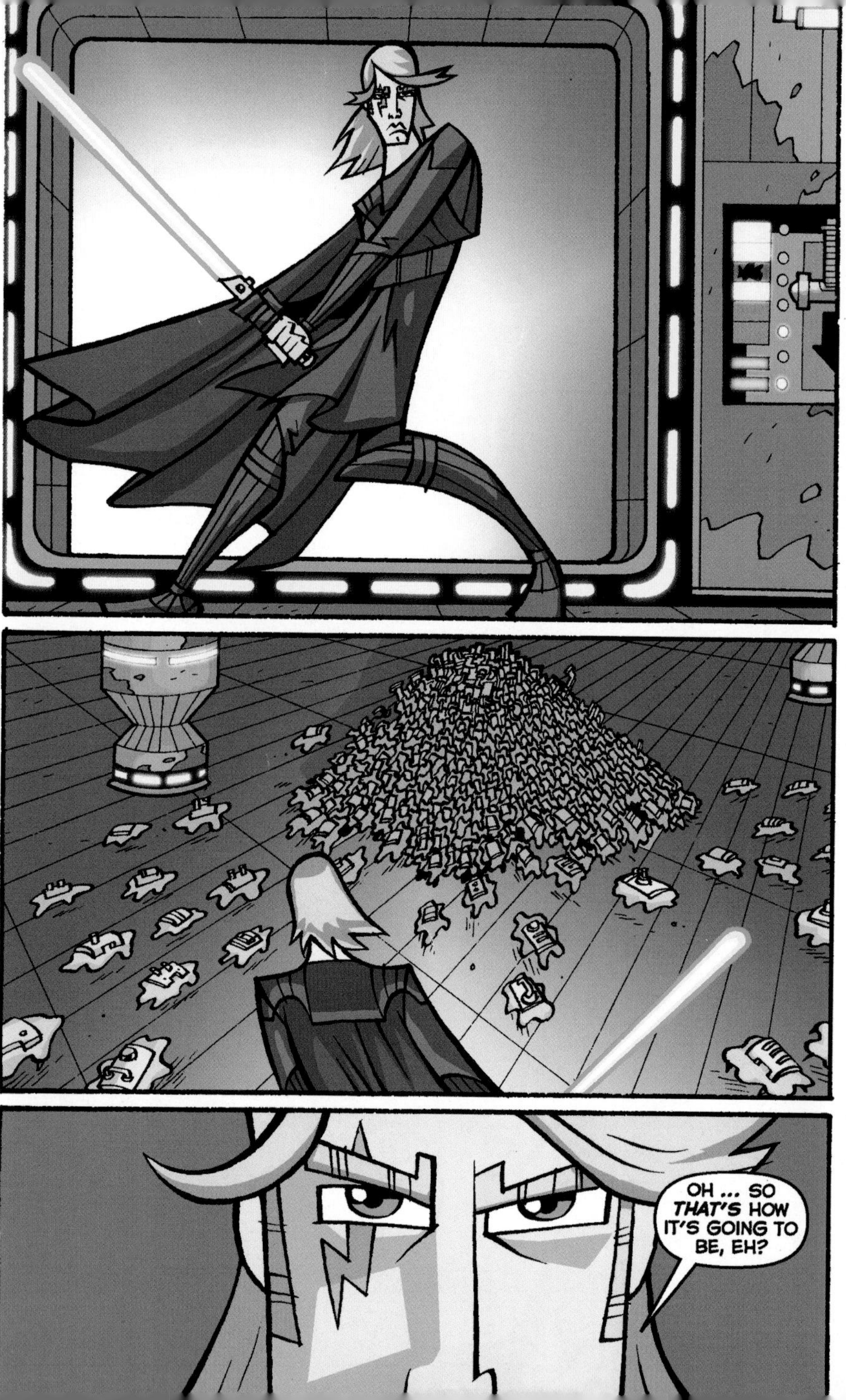
OH ... SO *THAT'S* HOW IT'S GOING TO BE, EH?

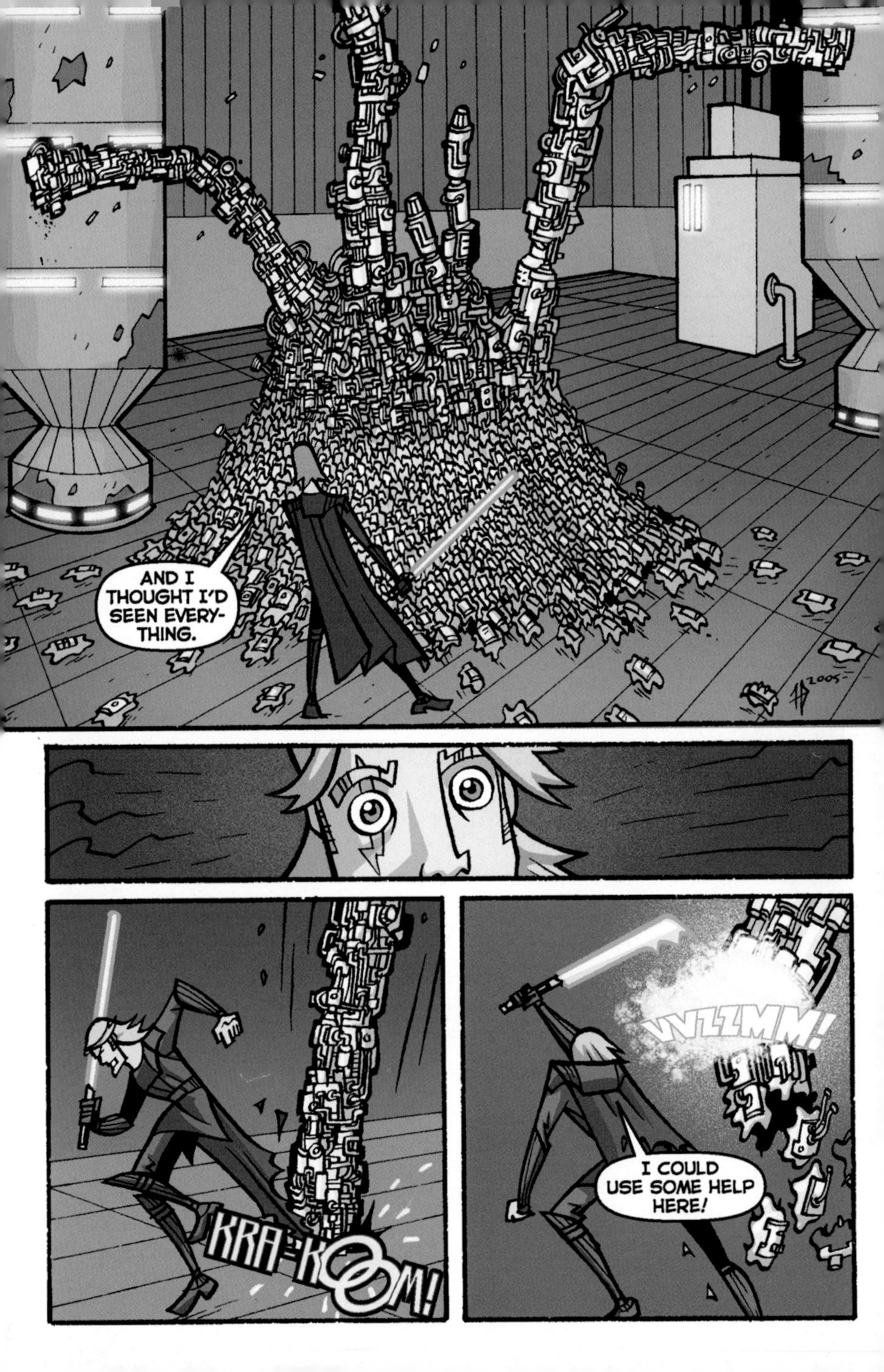
AND I THOUGHT I'D SEEN EVERY-THING.
KRA-KOOM!
VVZZMM!
I COULD USE SOME HELP HERE!

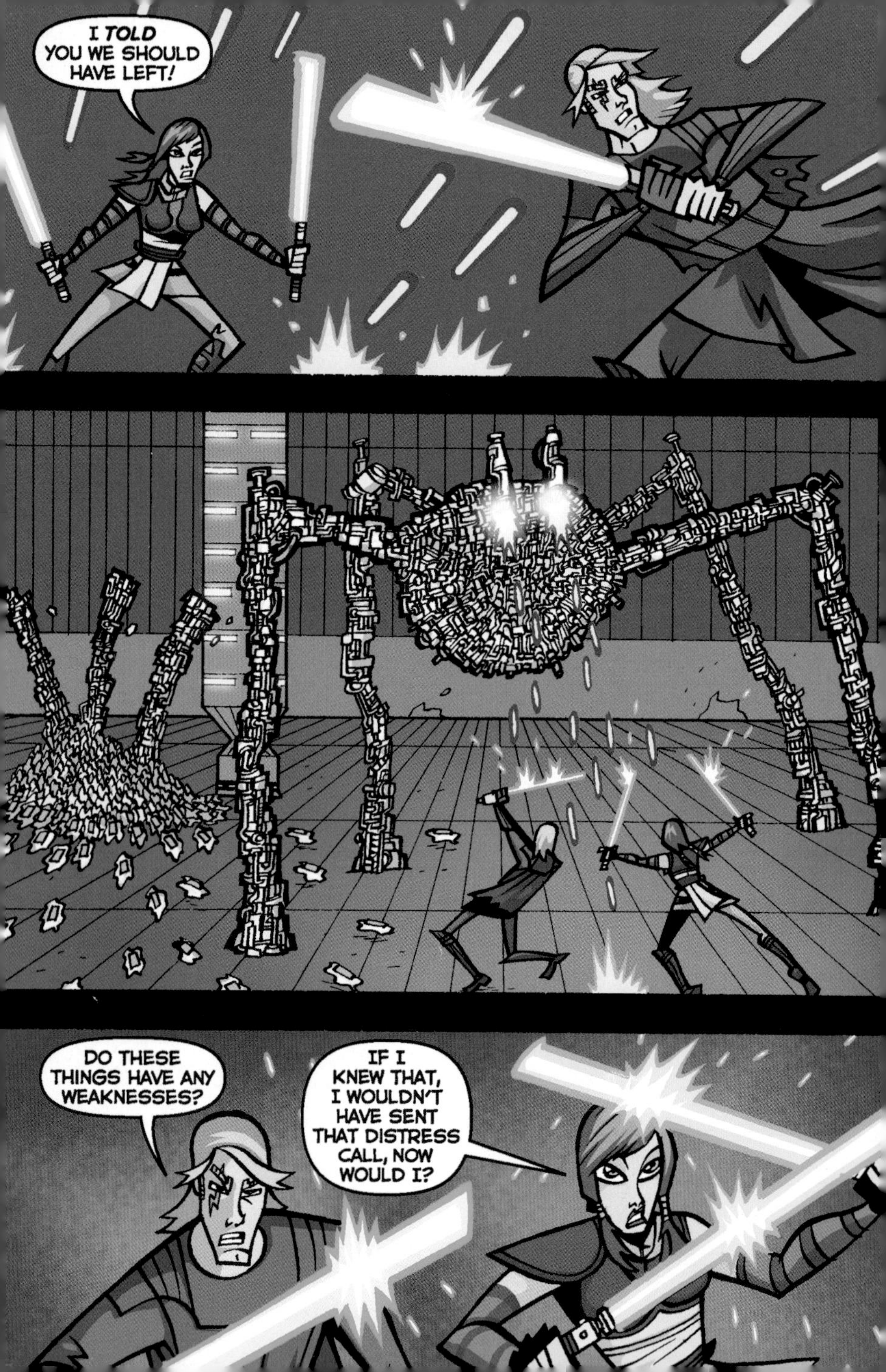
I TOLD YOU WE SHOULD HAVE LEFT!
DO THESE THINGS HAVE ANY WEAKNESSES?
IF I KNEW THAT, I WOULDN'T HAVE SENT THAT DISTRESS CALL, NOW WOULD I?

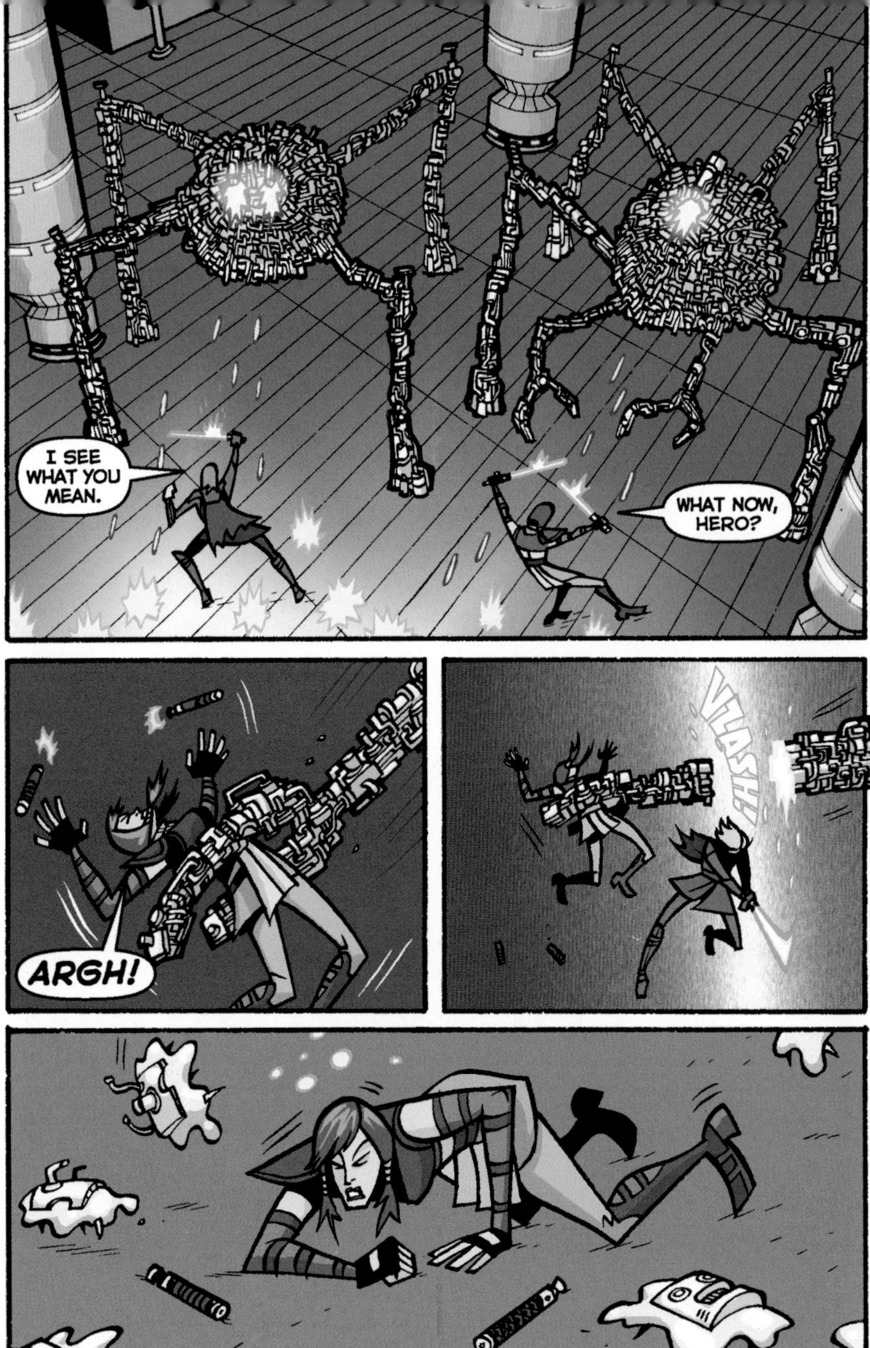
I SEE WHAT YOU MEAN.
WHAT NOW, HERO?
ARGH!
VLASH!

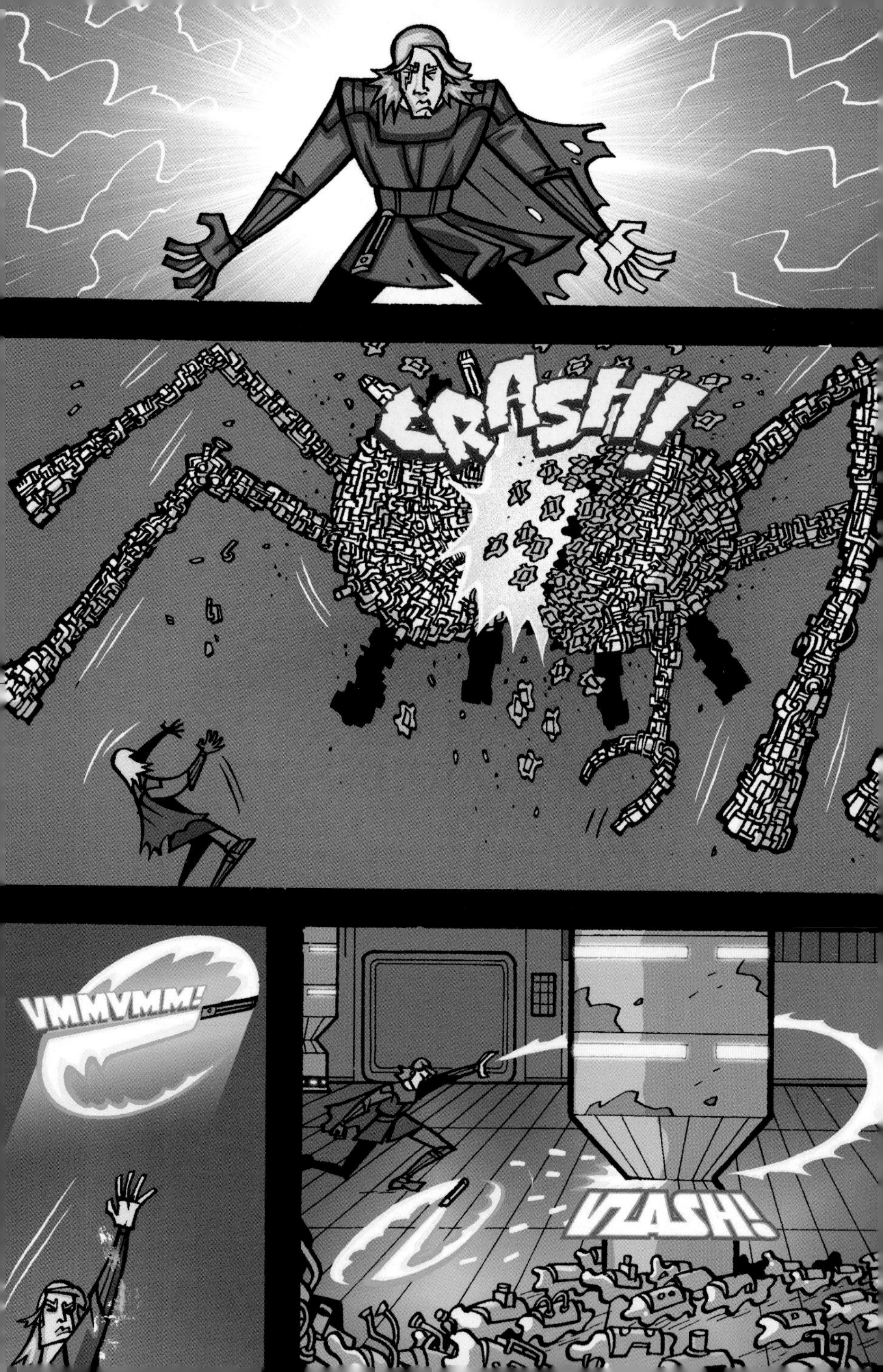
CRASH!!
VMMVMM!
VZASH!

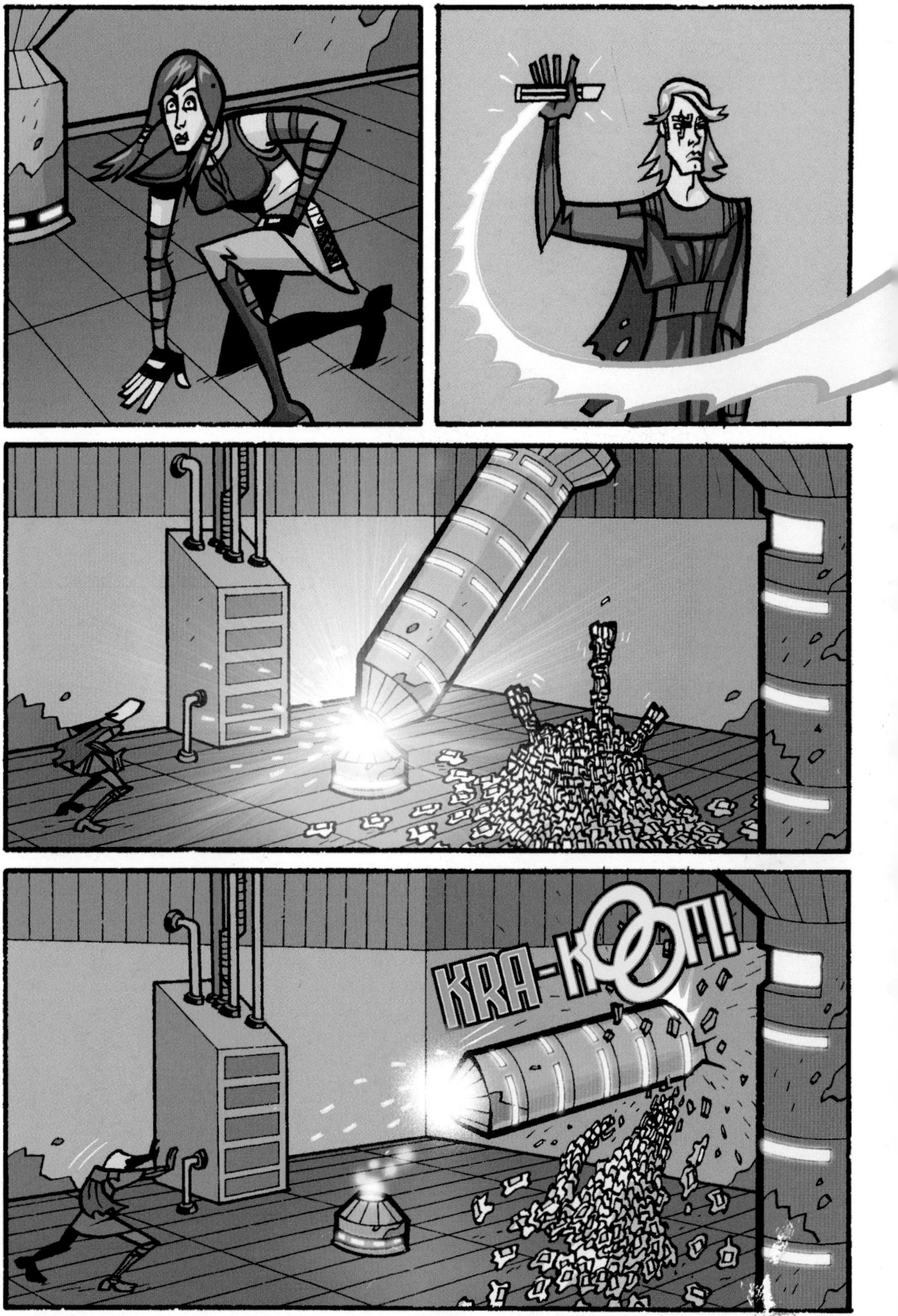
KRA-KOOM!

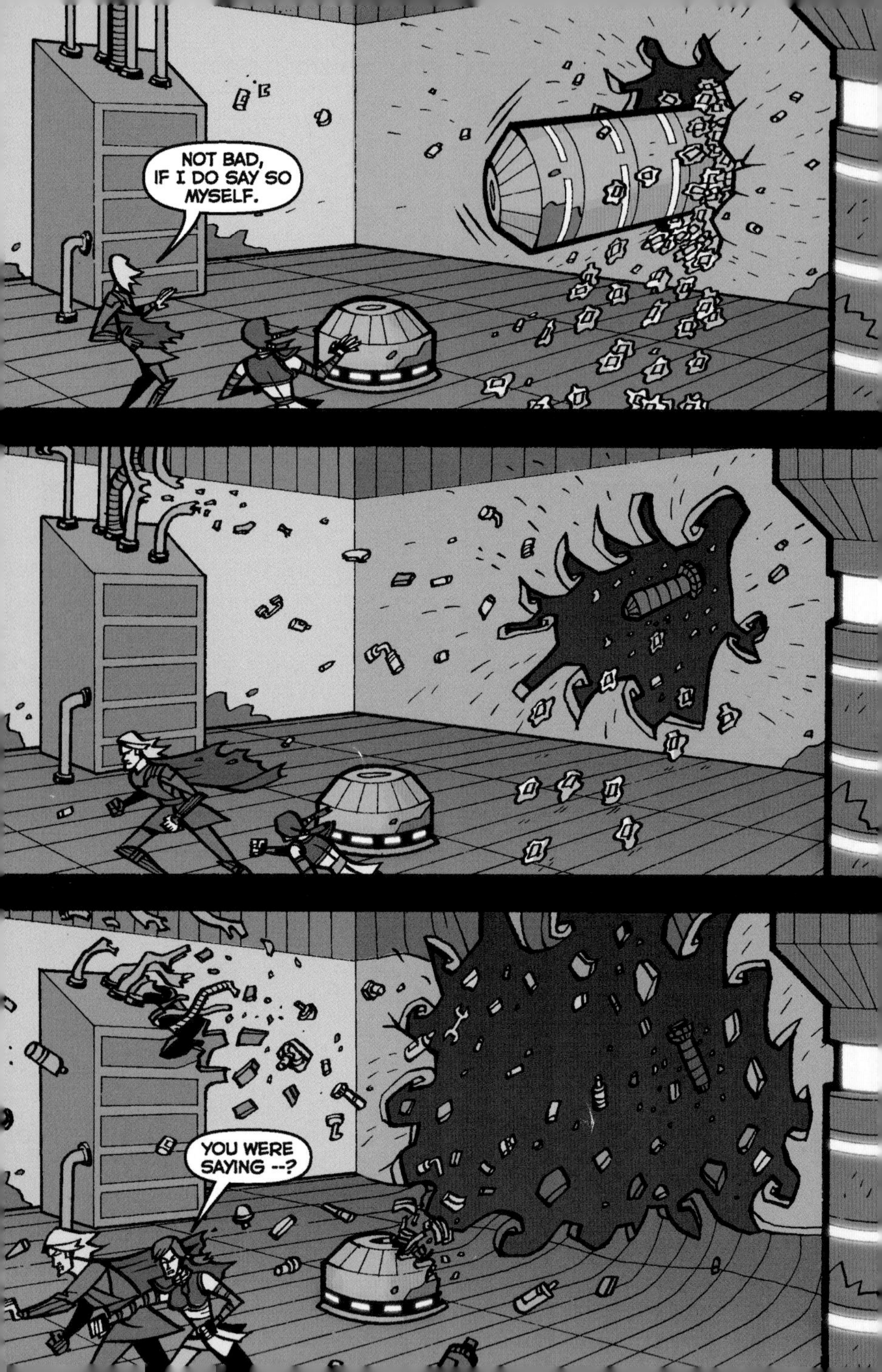
NOT BAD, IF I DO SAY SO MYSELF.
YOU WERE SAYING --?

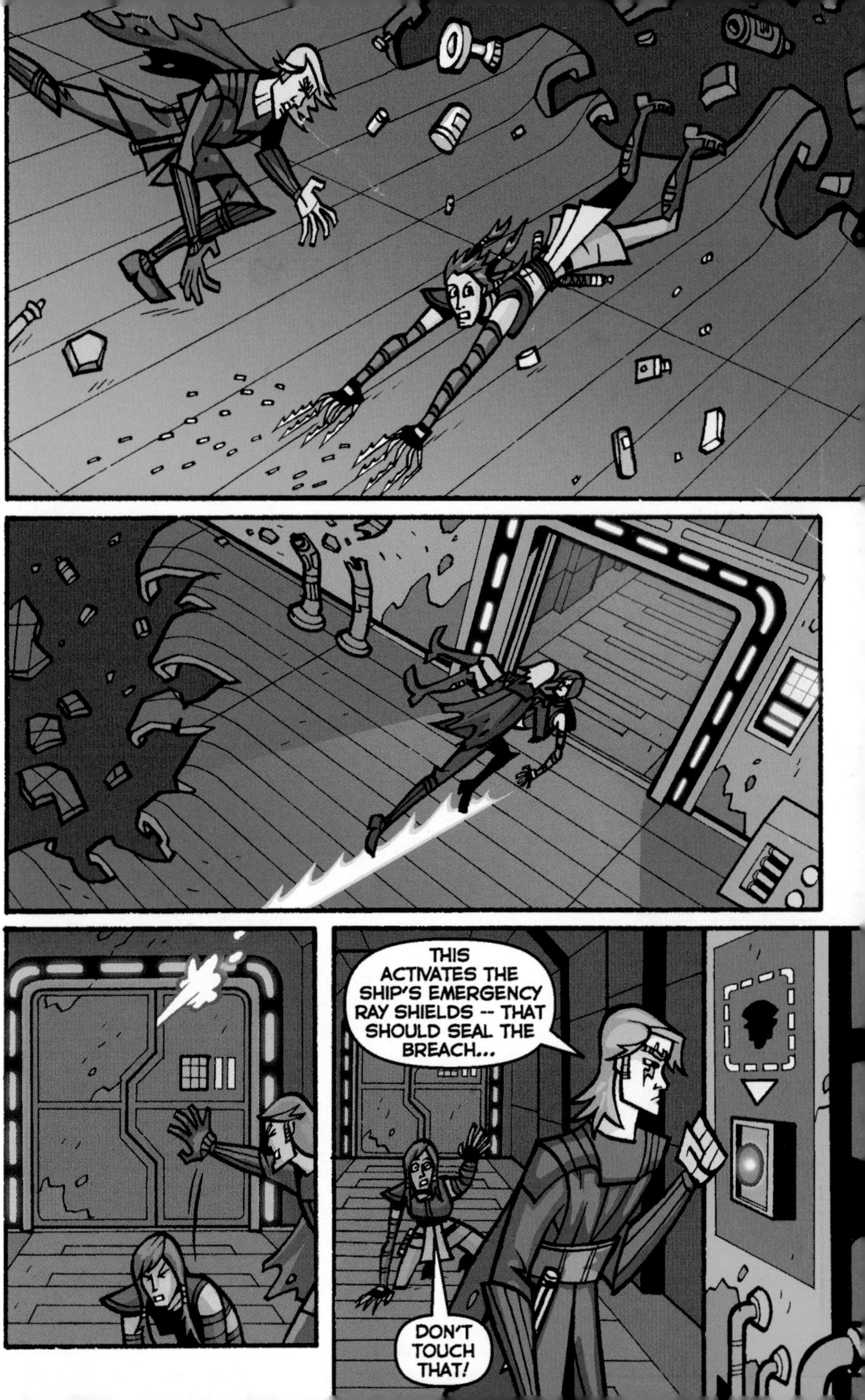
THIS ACTIVATES THE SHIP'S EMERGENCY RAY SHIELDS -- THAT SHOULD SEAL THE BREACH...
DON'T TOUCH THAT!

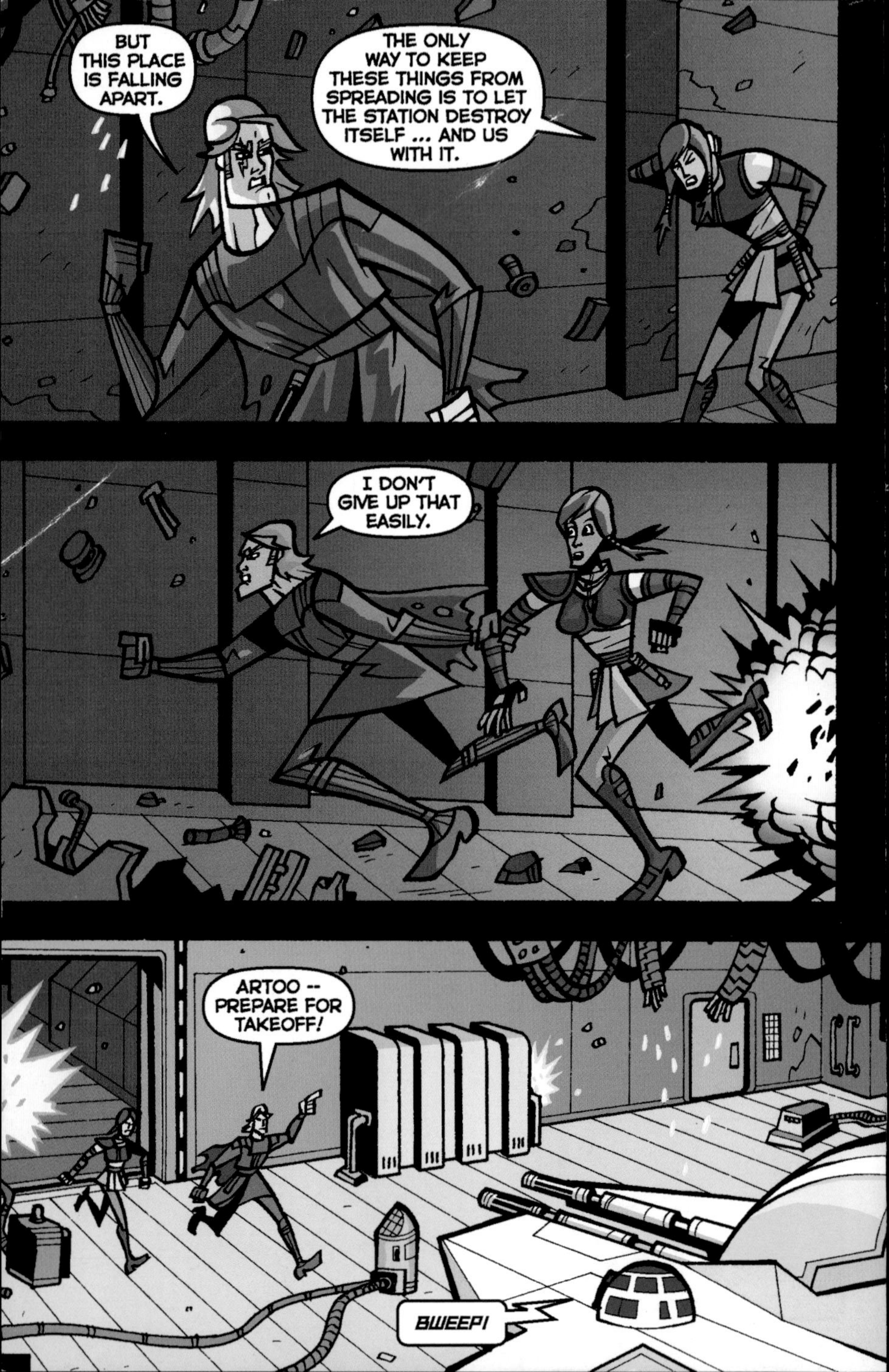
BUT THIS PLACE IS FALLING APART.
THE ONLY WAY TO KEEP THESE THINGS FROM SPREADING IS TO LET THE STATION DESTROY ITSELF ... AND US WITH IT.
I DON'T GIVE UP THAT EASILY.
ARTOO -- PREPARE FOR TAKEOFF!
BWEEP!

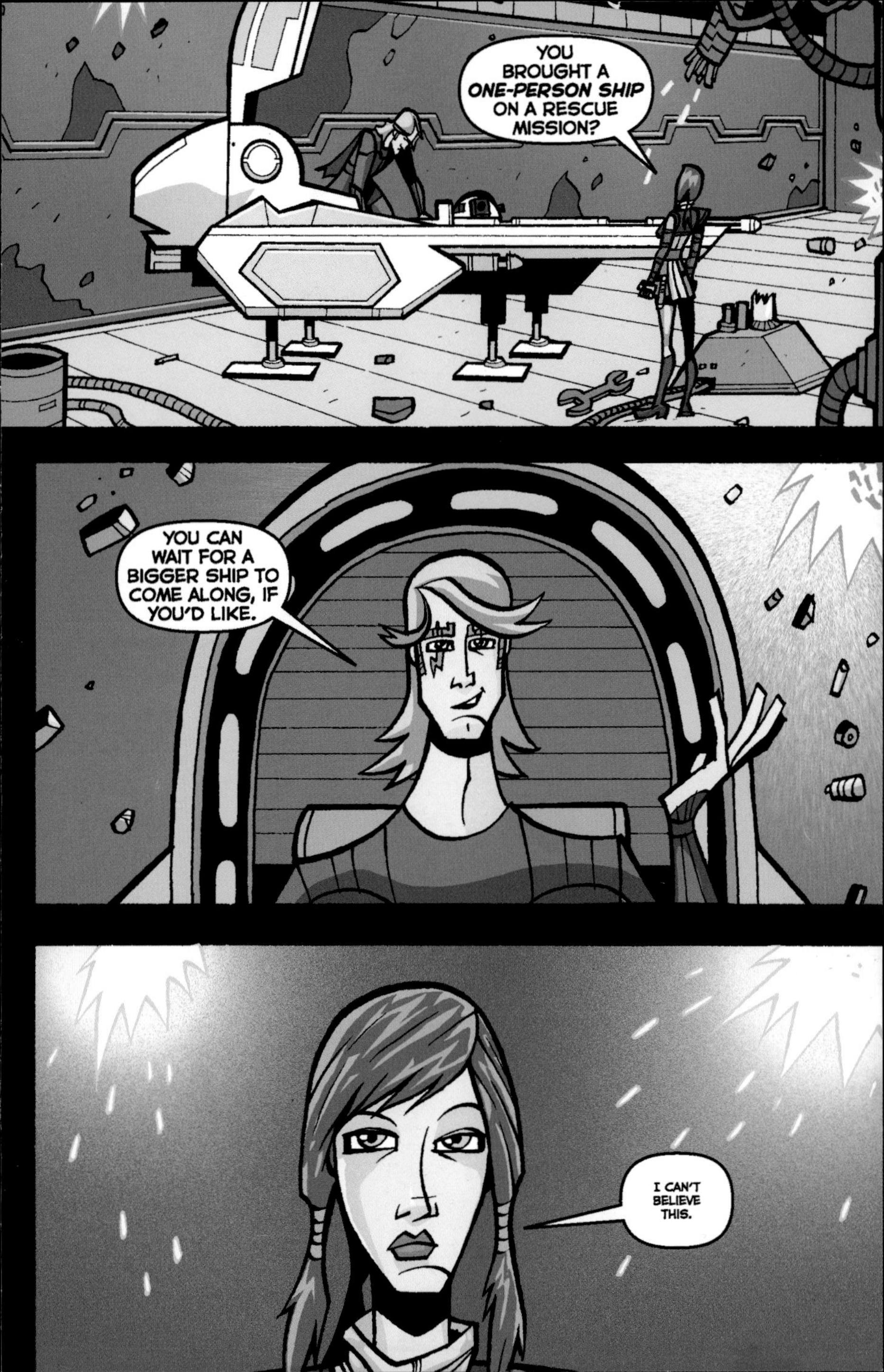
YOU BROUGHT A ONE-PERSON SHIP ON A RESCUE MISSION?
YOU CAN WAIT FOR A BIGGER SHIP TO COME ALONG, IF YOU'D LIKE.
I CAN'T BELIEVE THIS.

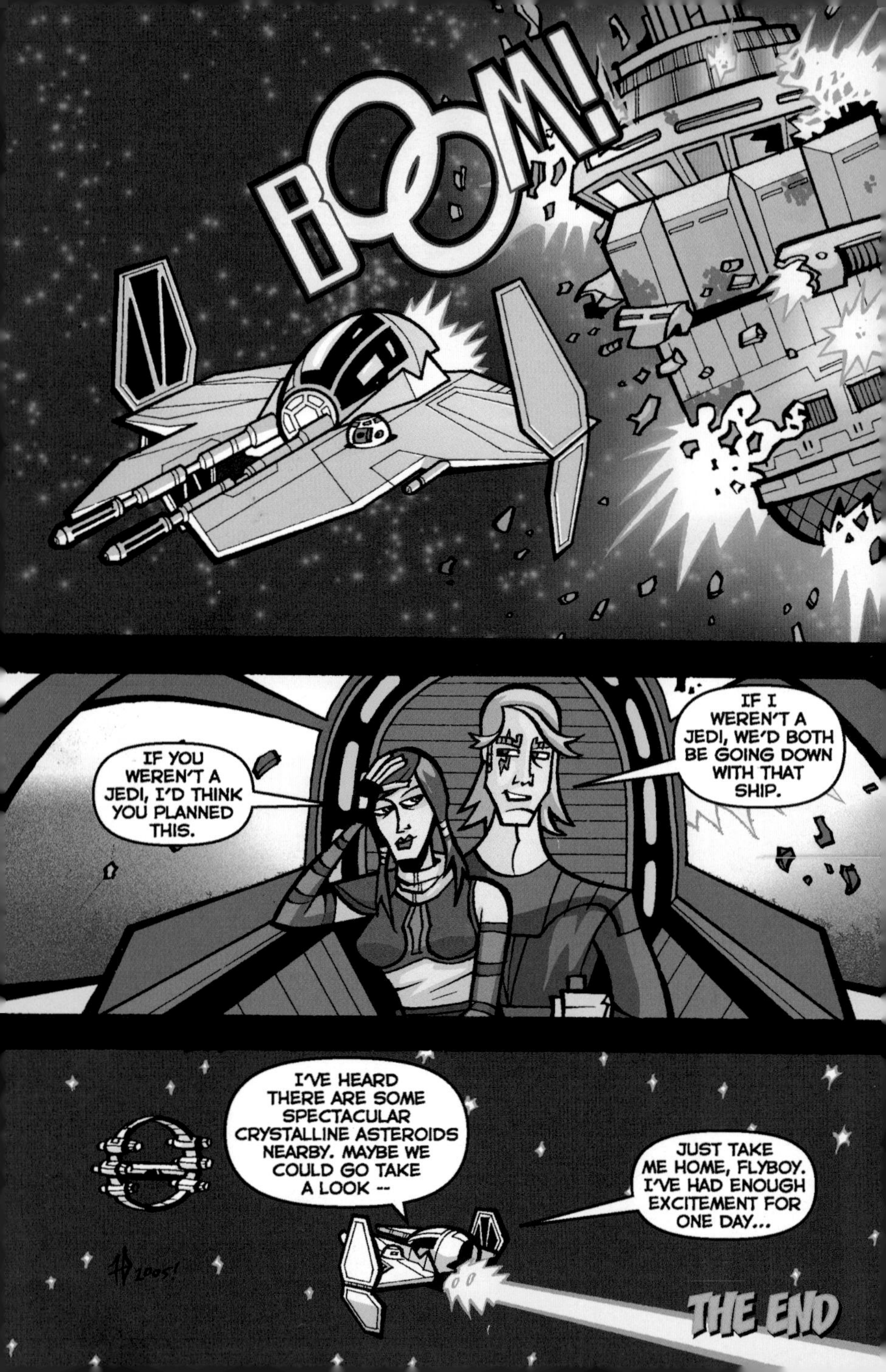
BOOM!
IF YOU WEREN'T A JEDI, I'D THINK YOU PLANNED THIS.
IF I WEREN'T A JEDI, WE'D BOTH BE GOING DOWN WITH THAT SHIP.
I'VE HEARD THERE ARE SOME SPECTACULAR CRYSTALLINE ASTEROIDS NEARBY. MAYBE WE COULD GO TAKE A LOOK --
JUST TAKE ME HOME, FLYBOY. I'VE HAD ENOUGH EXCITEMENT FOR ONE DAY...
THE END

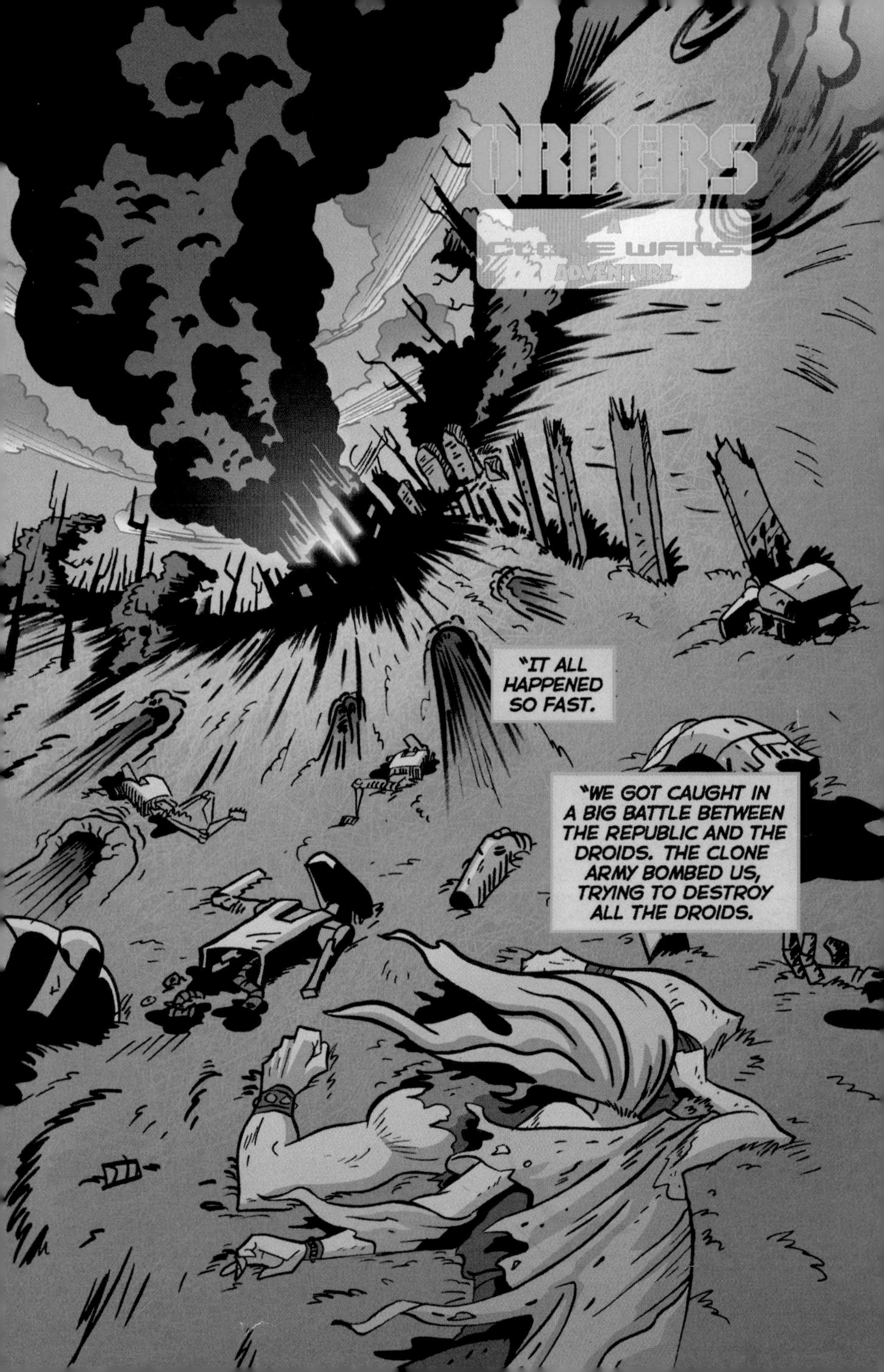
ORDERS
A CLONE WARS ADVENTURE
"IT ALL HAPPENED SO FAST.
"WE GOT CAUGHT IN A BIG BATTLE BETWEEN THE REPUBLIC AND THE DROIDS. THE CLONE ARMY BOMBED US, TRYING TO DESTROY ALL THE DROIDS.

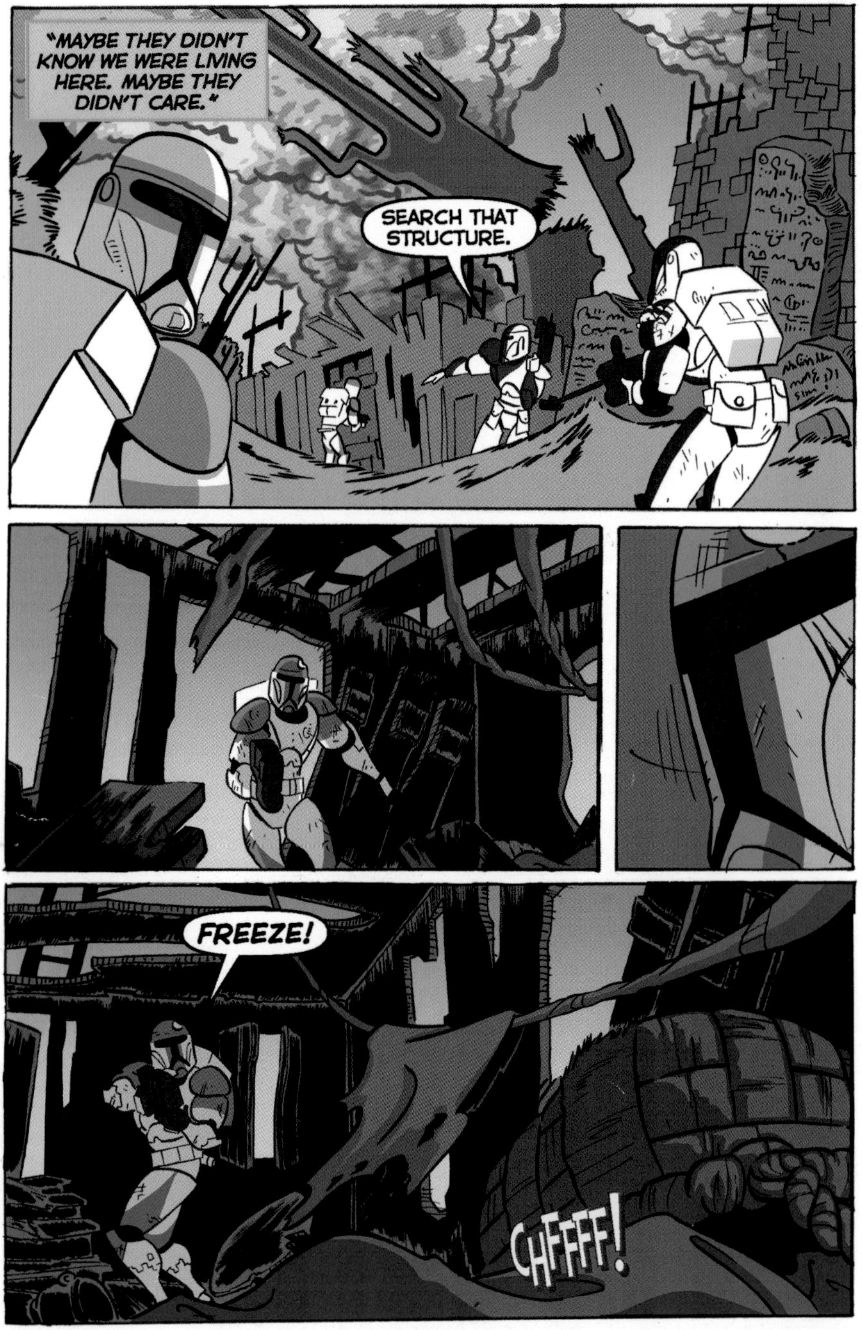
"MAYBE THEY DIDN'T KNOW WE WERE LIVING HERE. MAYBE THEY DIDN'T CARE."
SEARCH THAT STRUCTURE.
FREEZE!
CHFFFF!

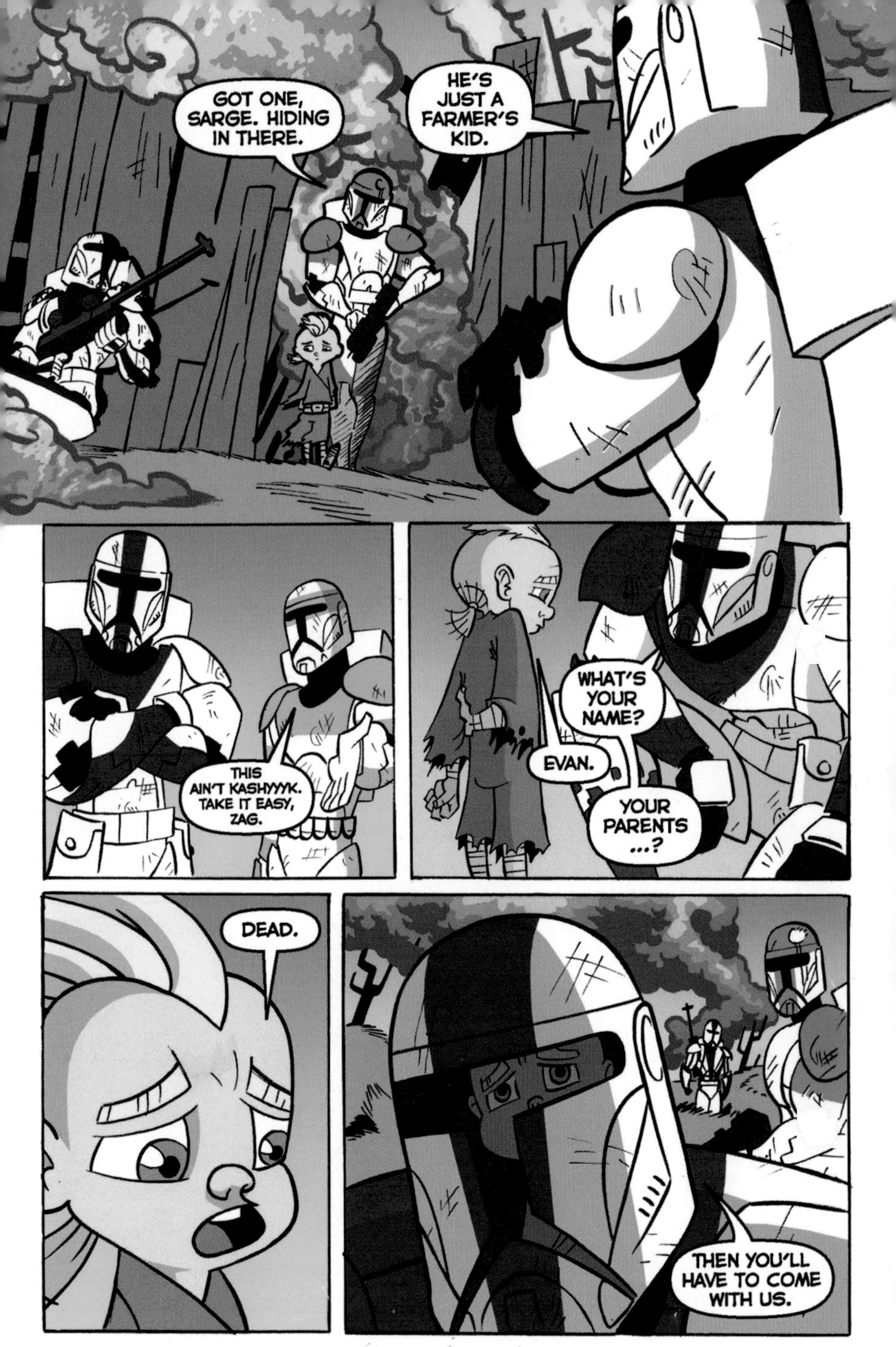

GOT ONE, SARGE. HIDING IN THERE.
HE'S JUST A FARMER'S KID.
THIS AIN'T KASHYYYK. TAKE IT EASY, ZAG.
WHAT'S YOUR NAME?
EVAN.
YOUR PARENTS ...?
DEAD.
THEN YOU'LL HAVE TO COME WITH US.

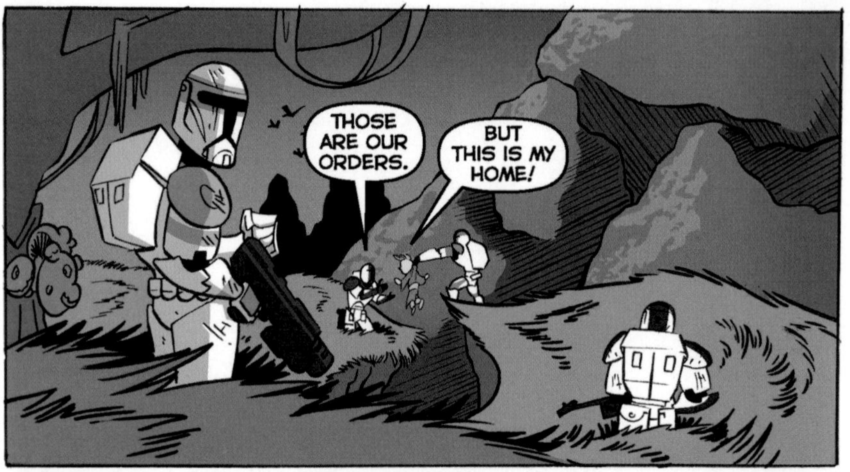
THOSE ARE OUR ORDERS.
BUT THIS IS MY HOME!

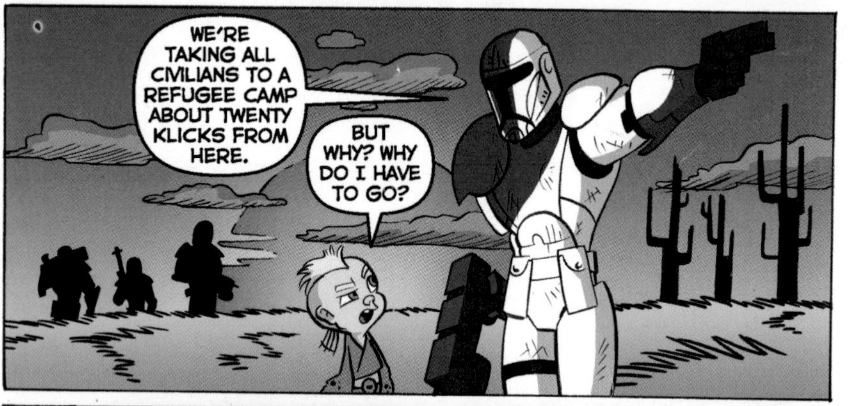
WE'RE TAKING ALL CIVILIANS TO A REFUGEE CAMP ABOUT TWENTY KLICKS FROM HERE.
BUT WHY? WHY DO I HAVE TO GO?

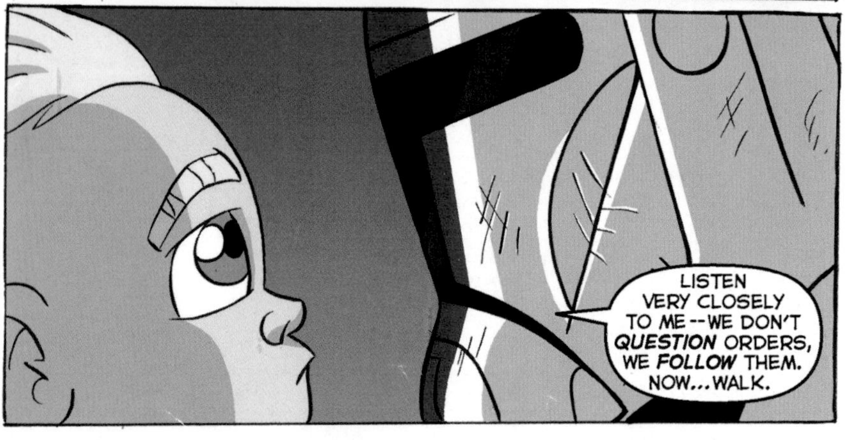
LISTEN VERY CLOSELY TO ME--WE DON'T *QUESTION* ORDERS, WE *FOLLOW* THEM. NOW...WALK.

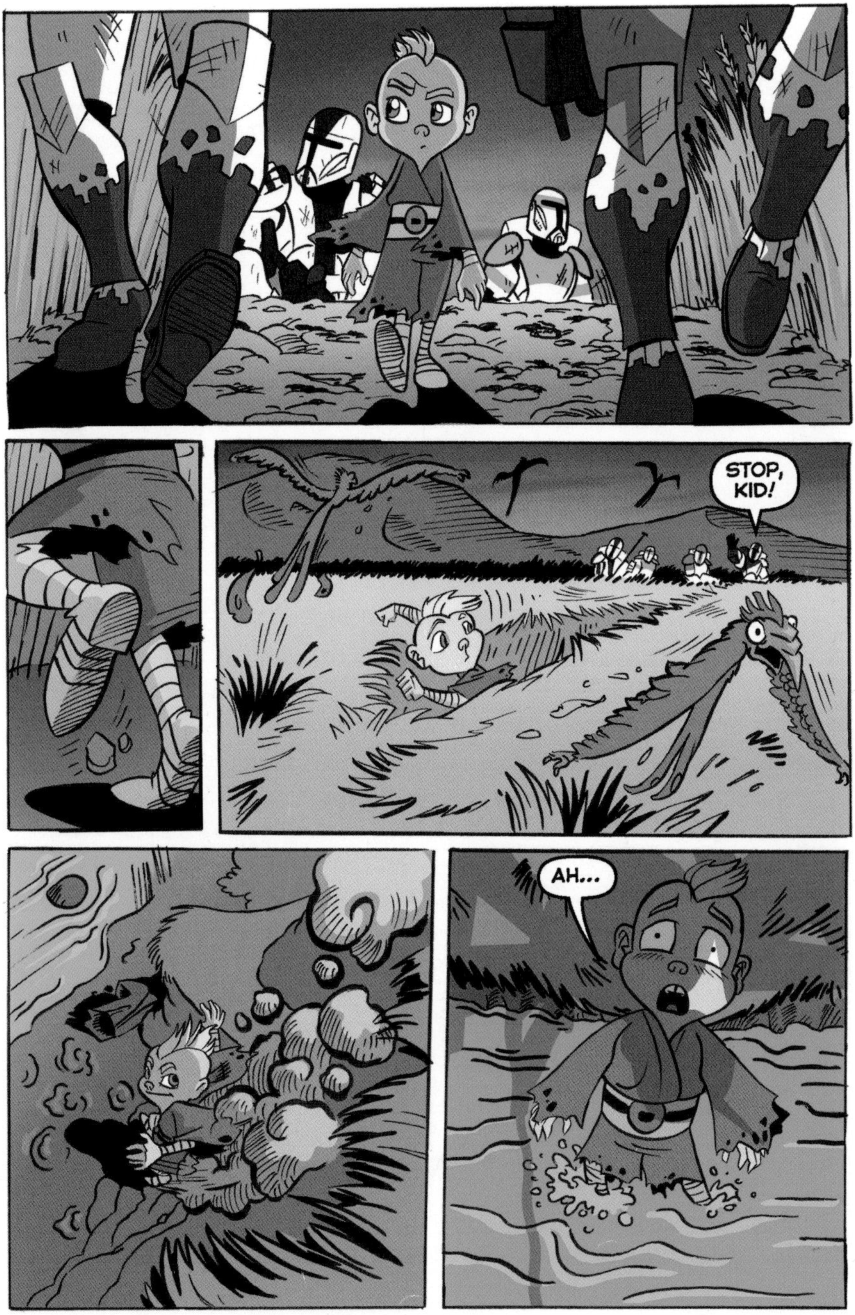
STOP, KID!
AH...

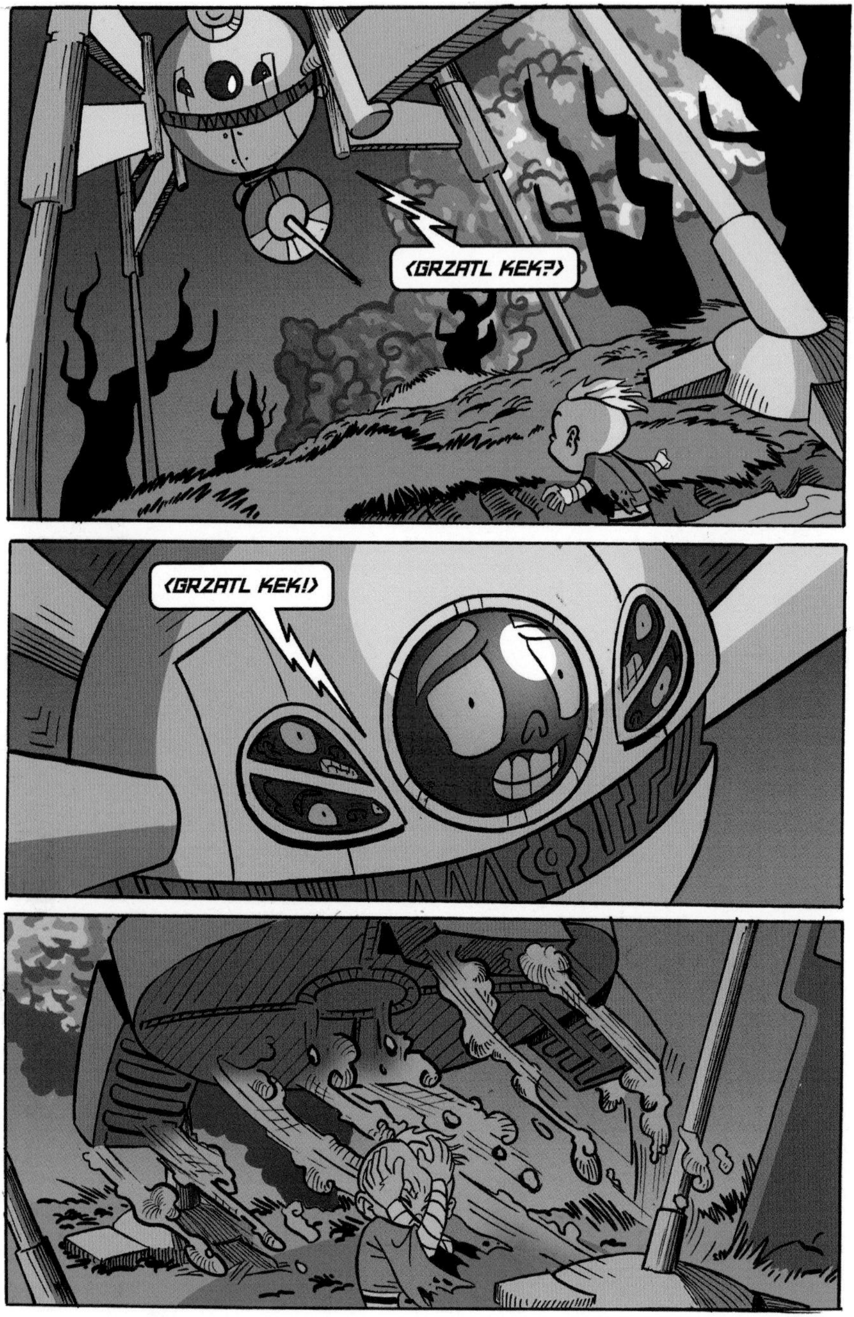
<GRZATL KEK?>
<GRZATL KEK!>

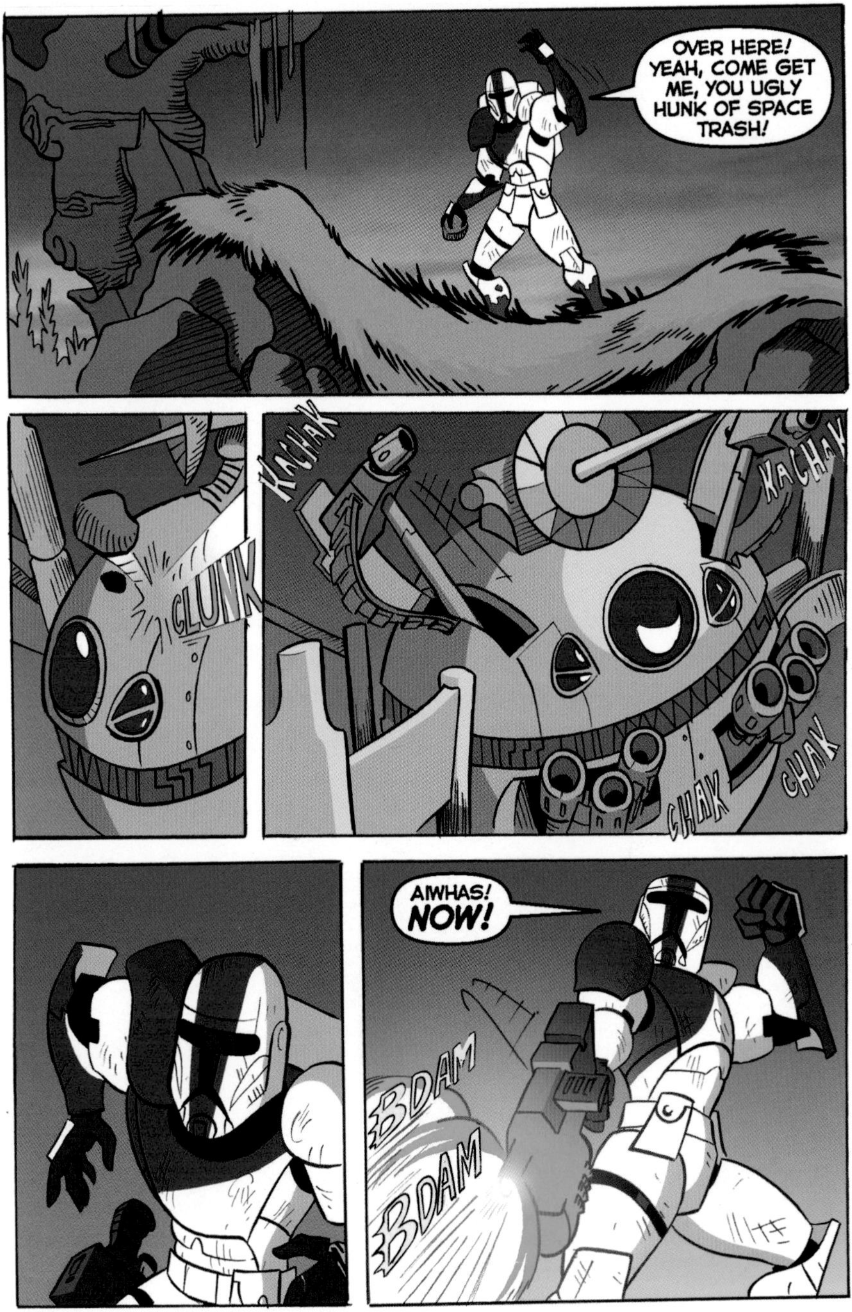
OVER HERE! YEAH, COME GET ME, YOU UGLY HUNK OF SPACE TRASH!
CLUNK
KACHAK
KACHAK
CHAK
CHAK
AIWHAS! NOW!
BDAM
BDAM

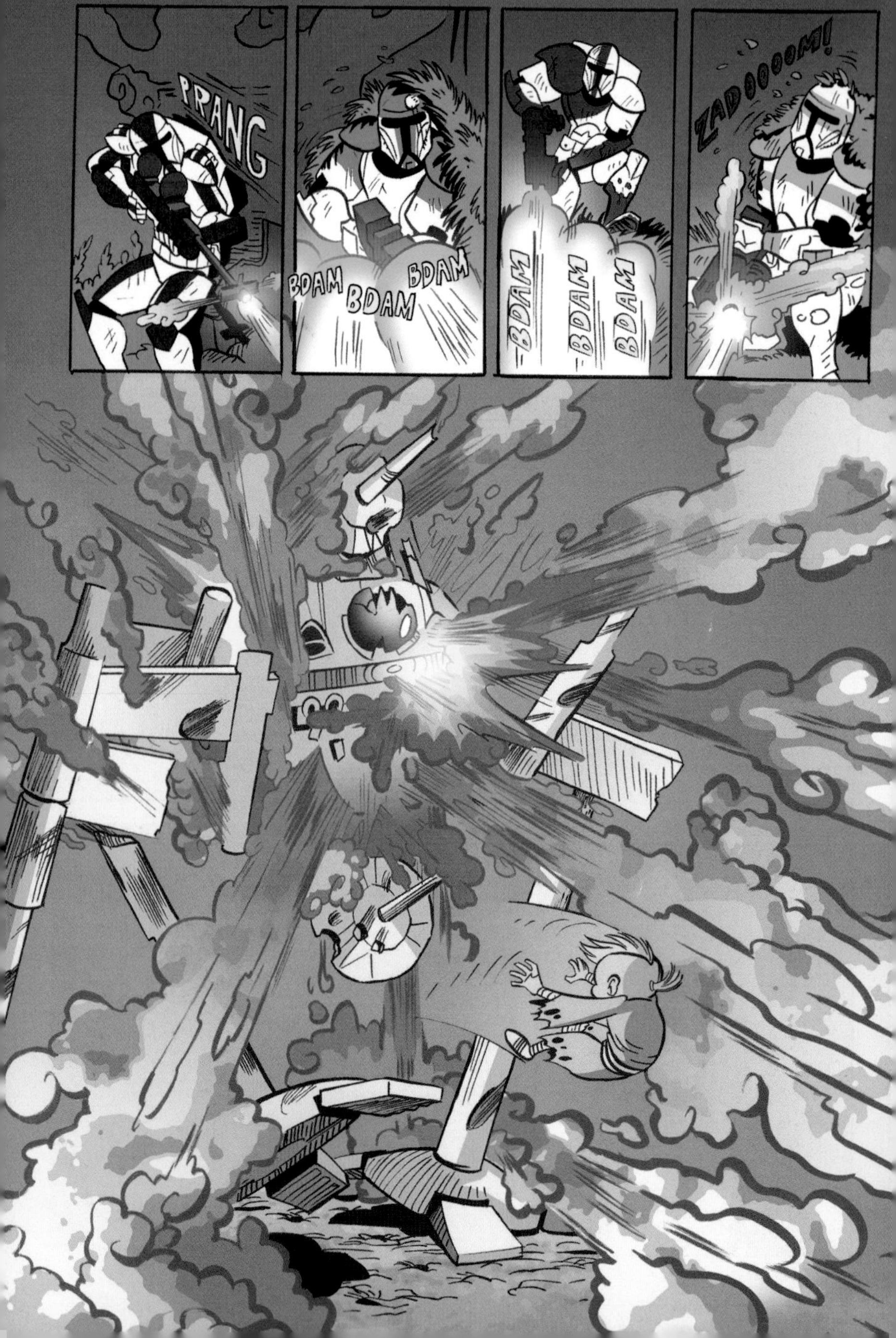
PRANG
BDAM
BDAM
BDAM
BDAM
BDAM
BDAM
ZADOOOOM!

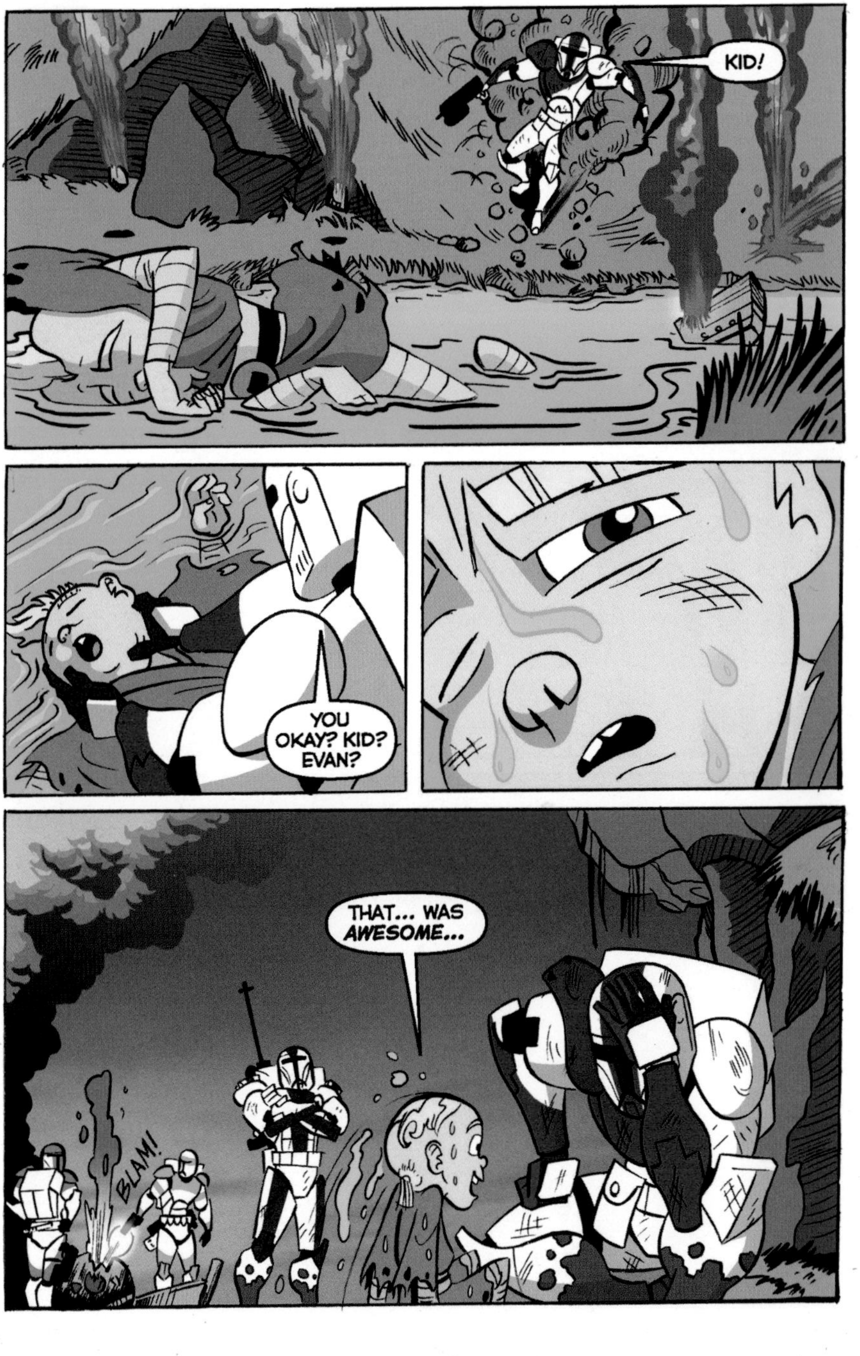
KID!
YOU OKAY? KID? EVAN?
THAT... WAS AWESOME...
BLAM!

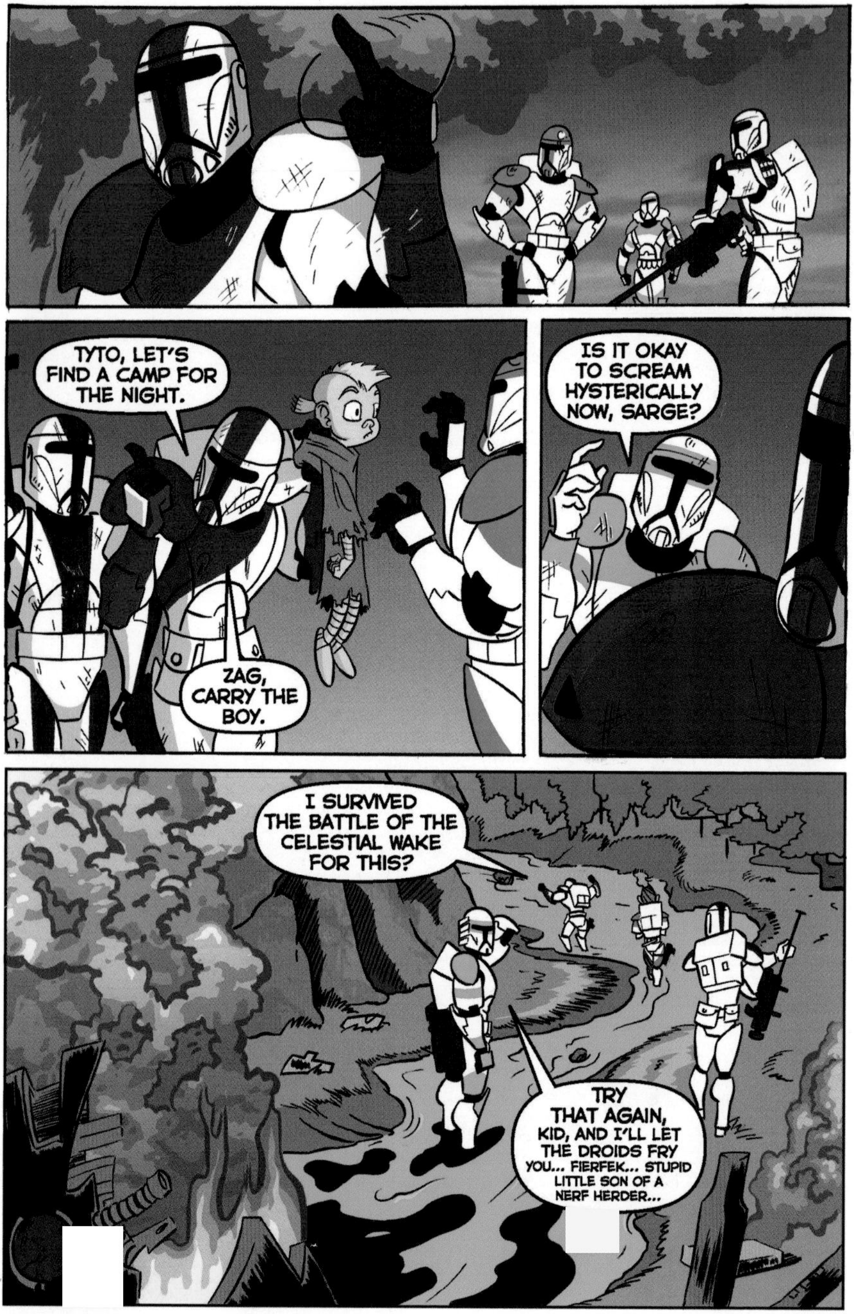
TYTO, LET'S FIND A CAMP FOR THE NIGHT.
ZAG, CARRY THE BOY.
IS IT OKAY TO SCREAM HYSTERICALLY NOW, SARGE?
I SURVIVED THE BATTLE OF THE CELESTIAL WAKE FOR THIS?
TRY THAT AGAIN, KID, AND I'LL LET THE DROIDS FRY YOU... FIERFEK... STUPID LITTLE SON OF A NERF HERDER...

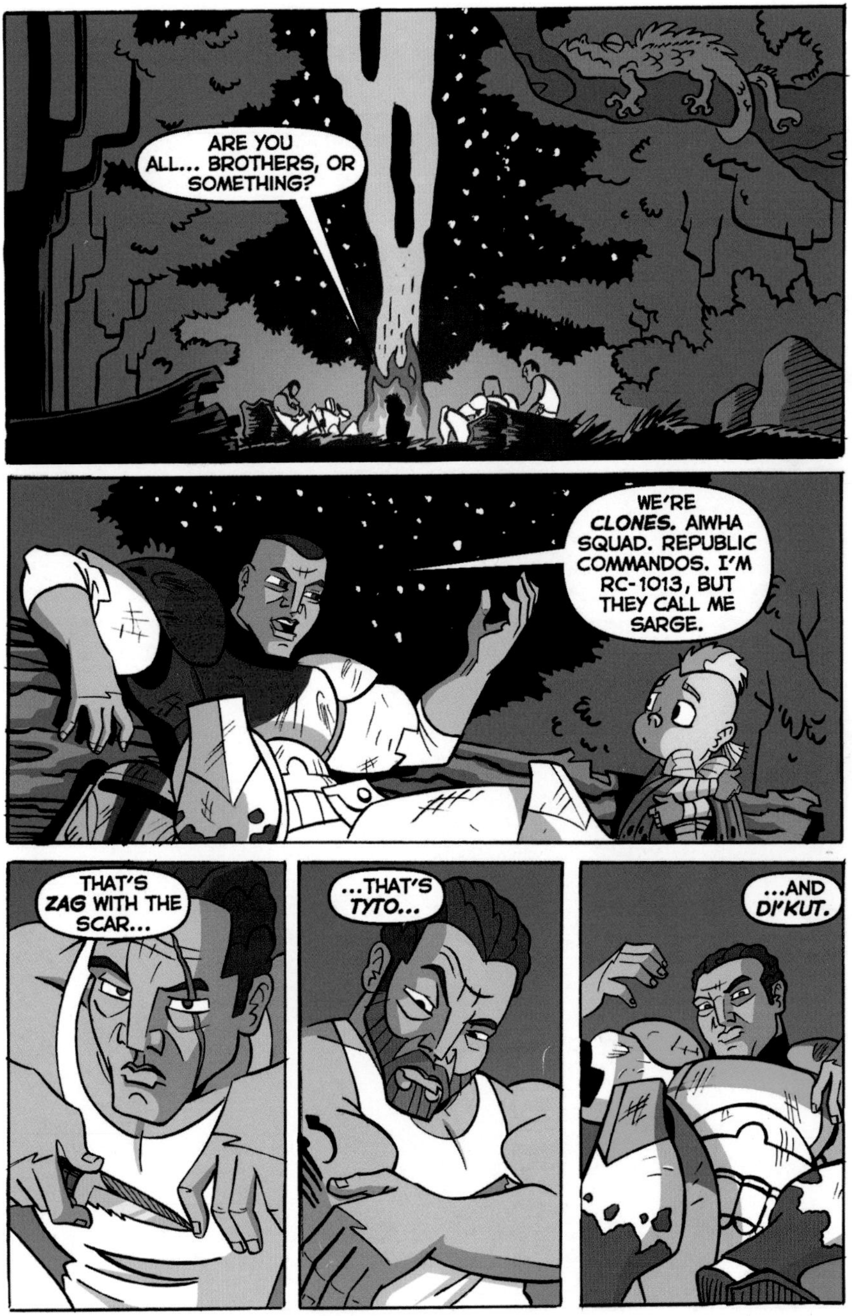
ARE YOU ALL... BROTHERS, OR SOMETHING?
WE'RE *CLONES.* AIWHA SQUAD. REPUBLIC COMMANDOS. I'M RC-1013, BUT THEY CALL ME SARGE.
THAT'S ZAG WITH THE SCAR...
...THAT'S *TYTO*...
...AND *DI'KUT*.

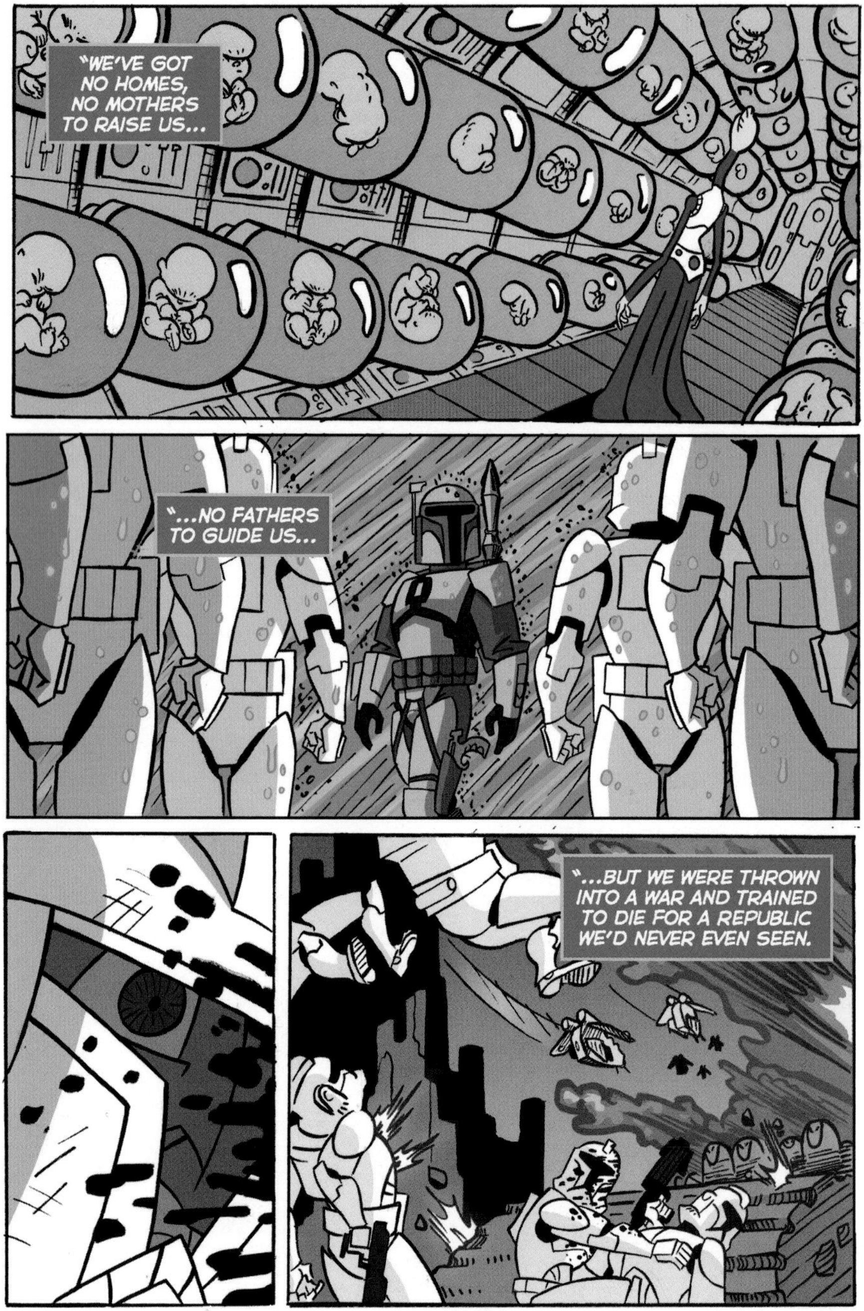
"WE'VE GOT NO HOMES, NO MOTHERS TO RAISE US...
"...NO FATHERS TO GUIDE US...
"...BUT WE WERE THROWN INTO A WAR AND TRAINED TO DIE FOR A REPUBLIC WE'D NEVER EVEN SEEN.

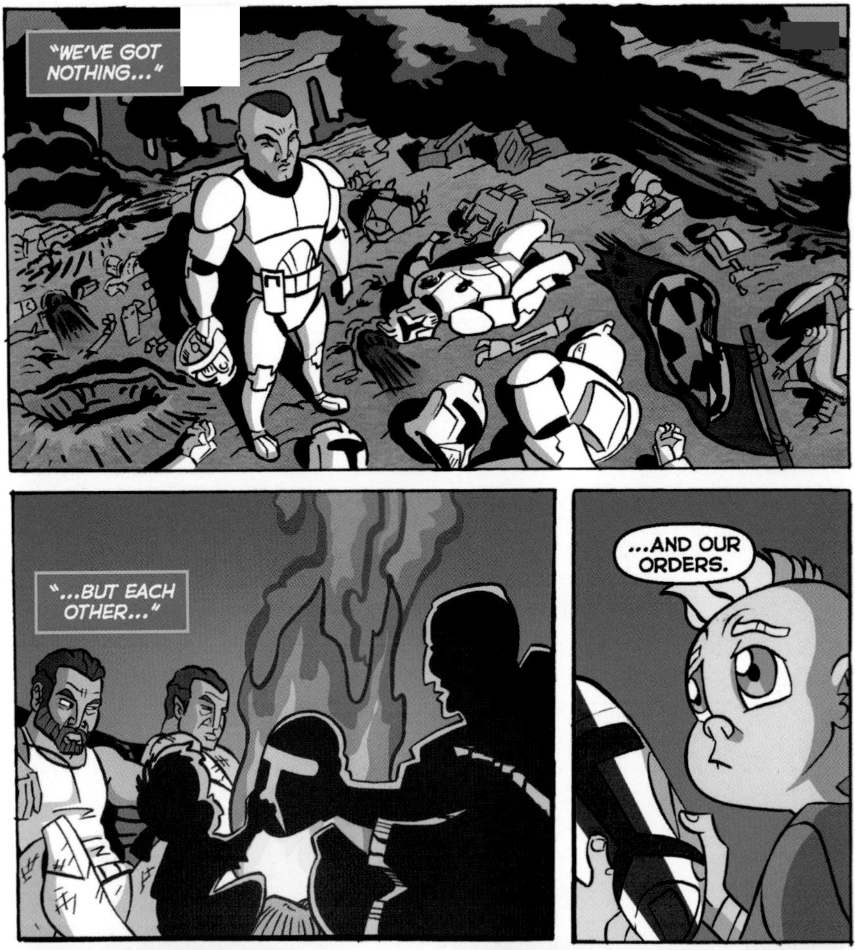
"WE'VE GOT NOTHING..."
"...BUT EACH OTHER..."
...AND OUR ORDERS.

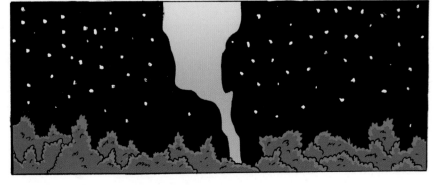

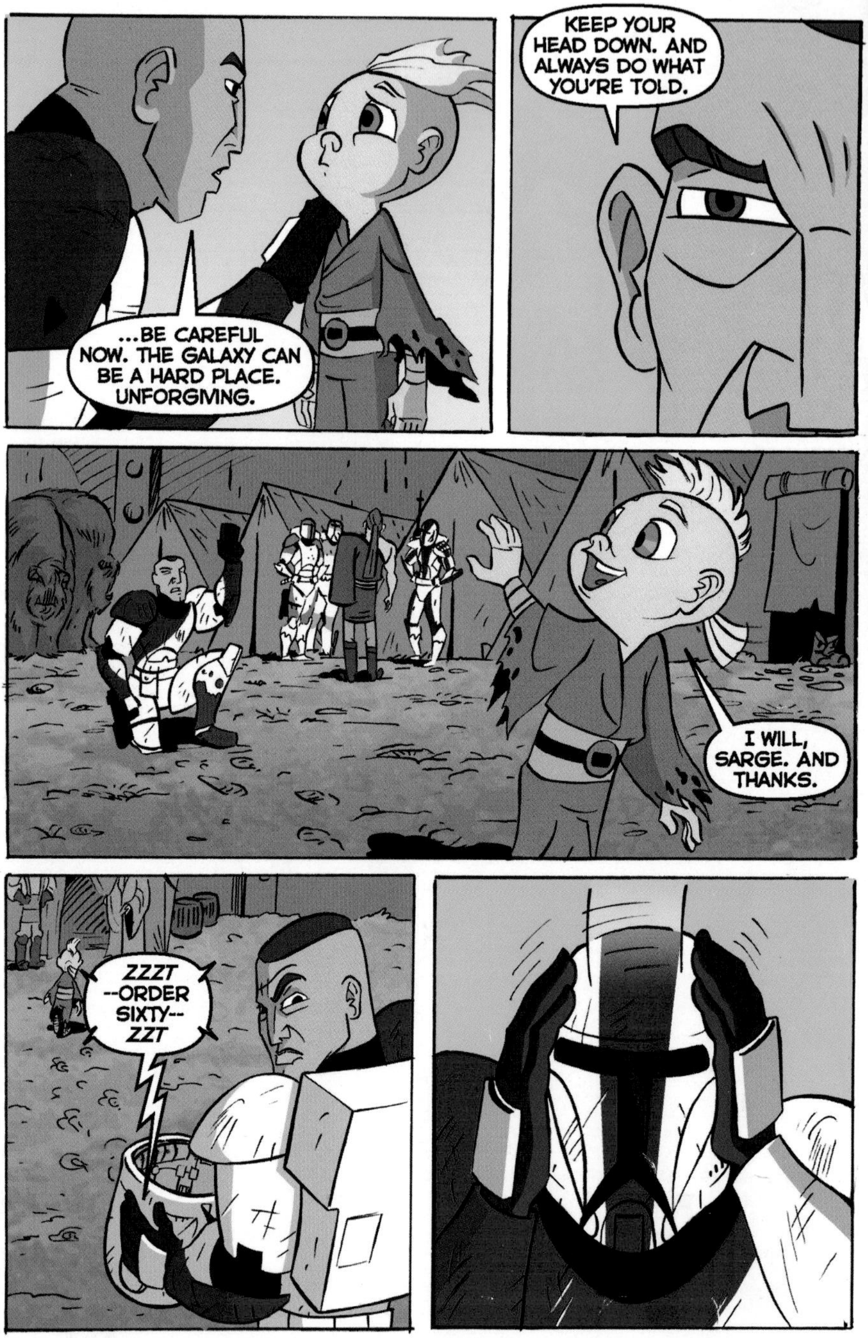
...BE CAREFUL NOW. THE GALAXY CAN BE A HARD PLACE. UNFORGIVING.
KEEP YOUR HEAD DOWN. AND ALWAYS DO WHAT YOU'RE TOLD.
I WILL, SARGE. AND THANKS.
ZZZT --ORDER SIXTY-- ZZT

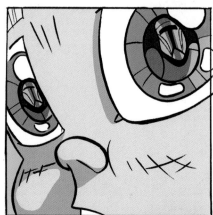

THE JEDI WERE TRAITORS TO THE REPUBLIC. WE FOLLOWED OUR ORDERS.

AND WE DON'T QUESTION ORDERS...

THE END

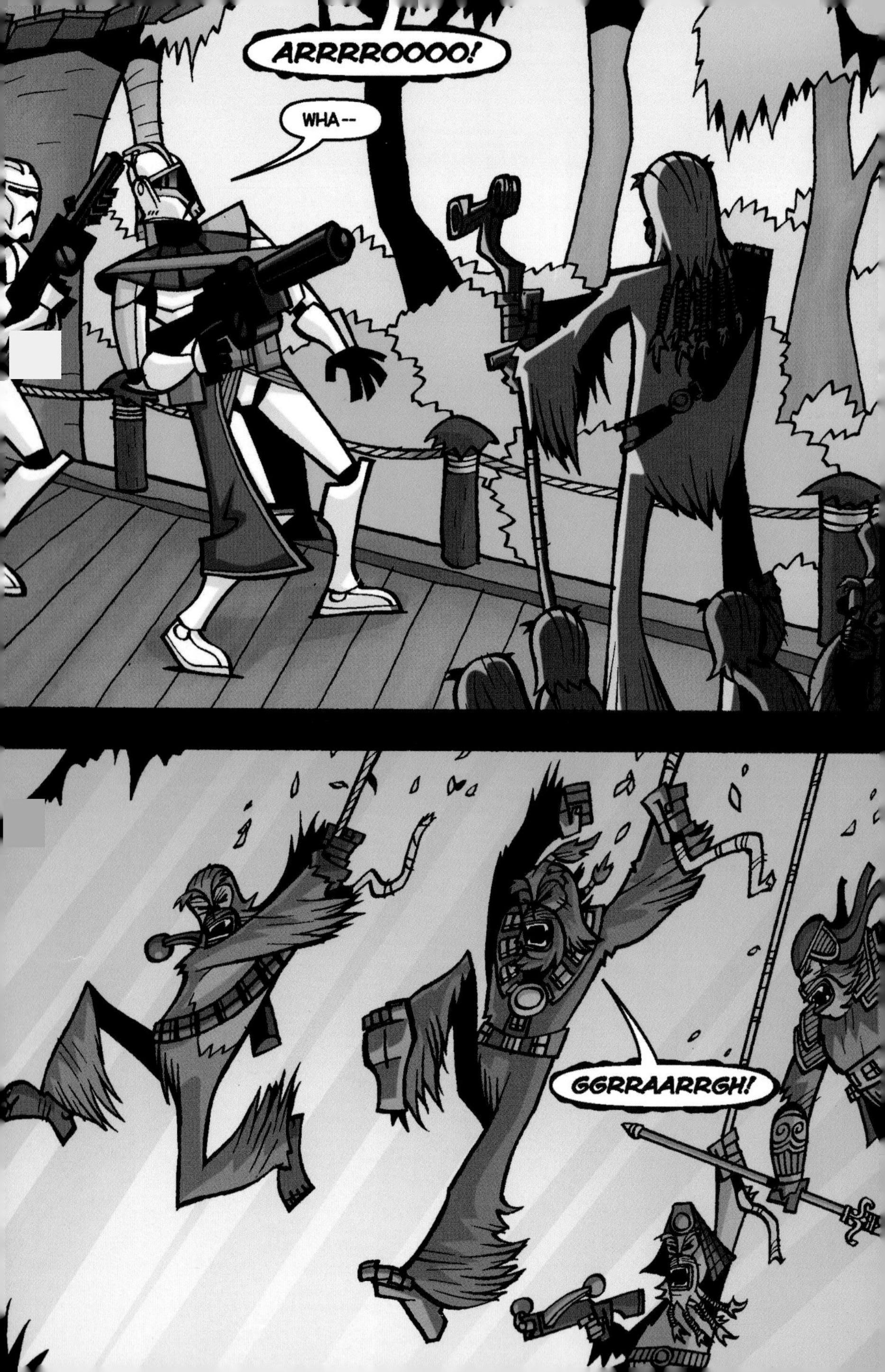
ARRRROOOO!
WHA--
GGRRAARRGH!

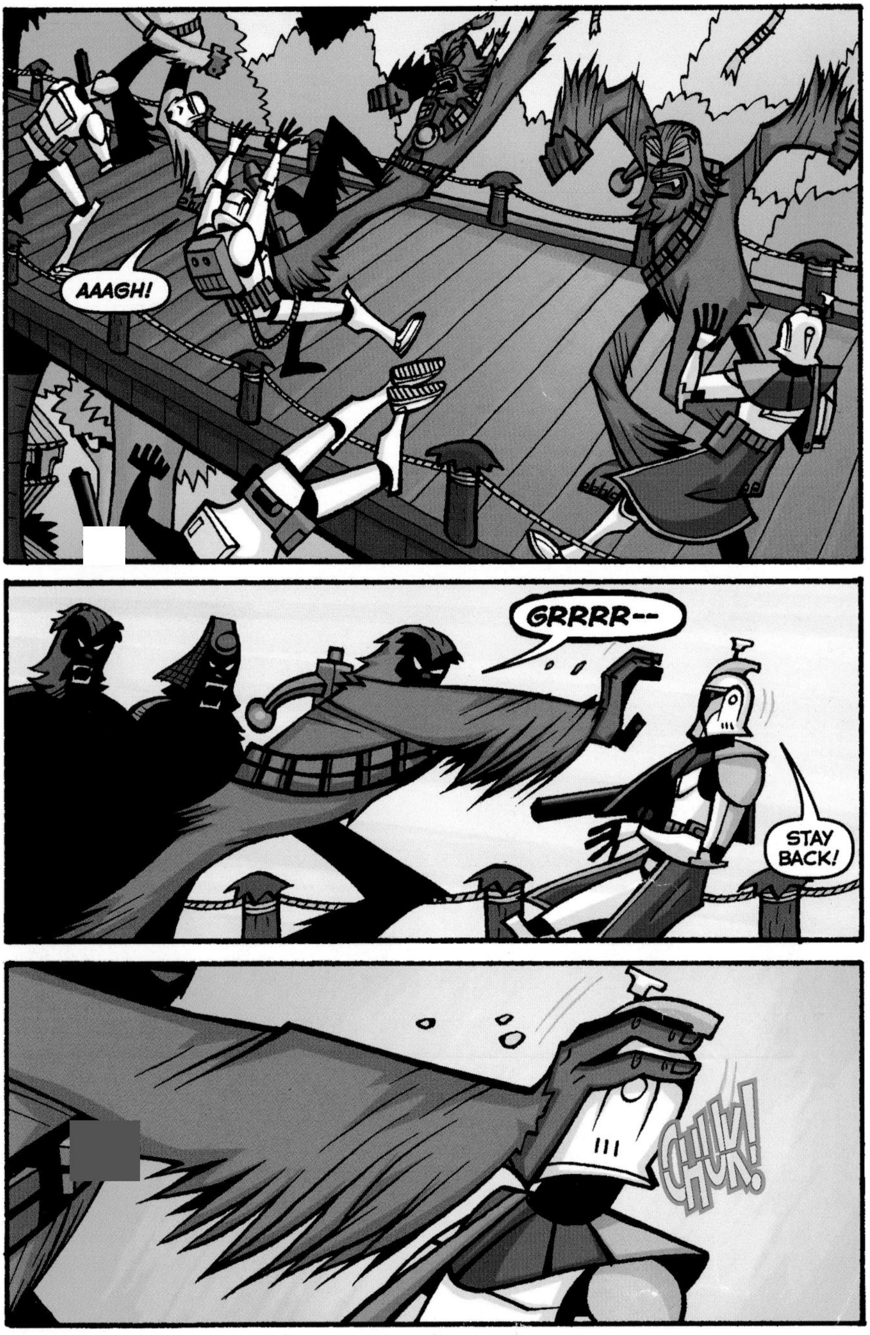
AAAGH!
GRRRR--
STAY BACK!
CHUK!

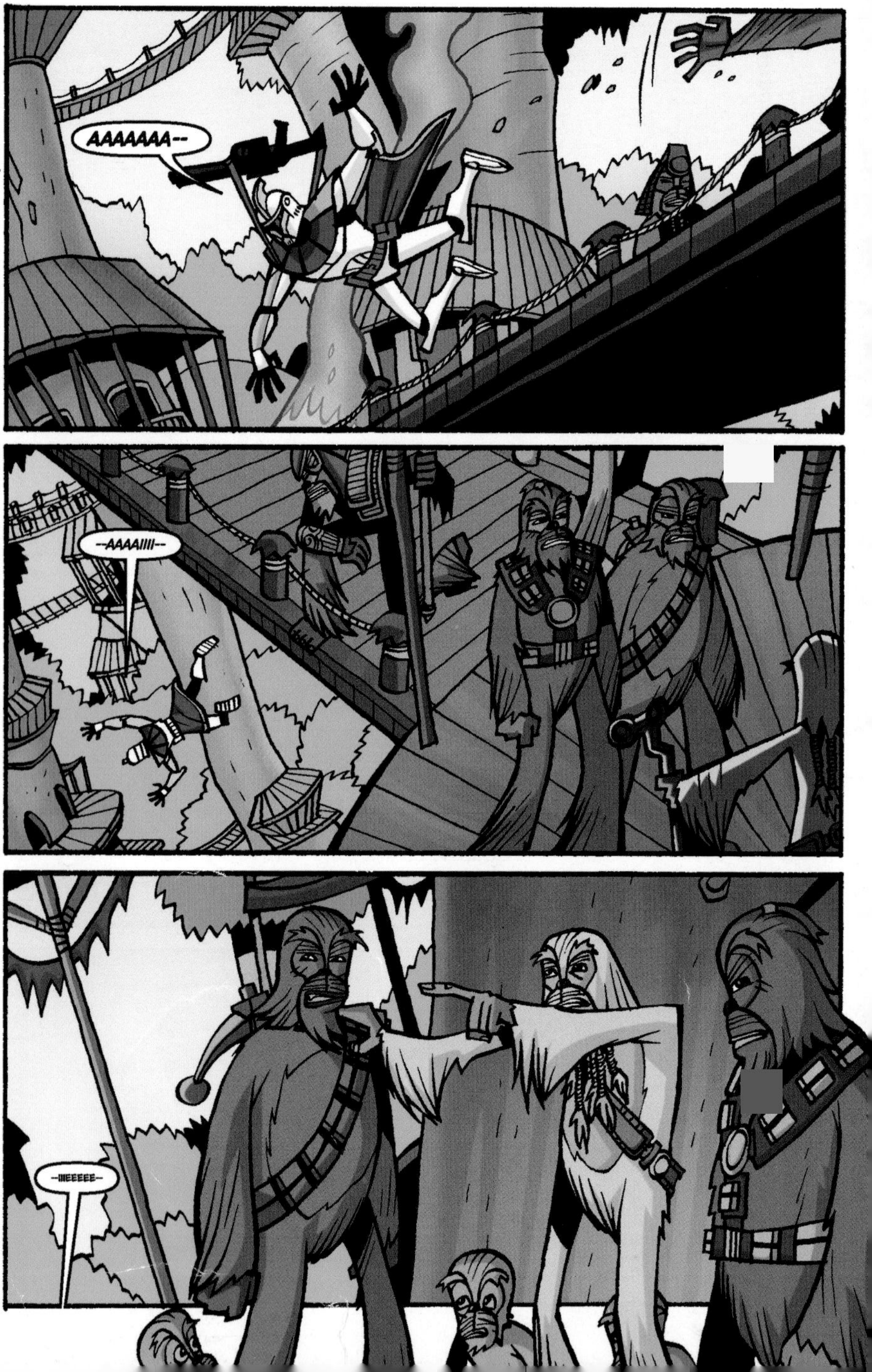
AAAAAAA--
--AAAAIIII--
--IIIEEEEE--

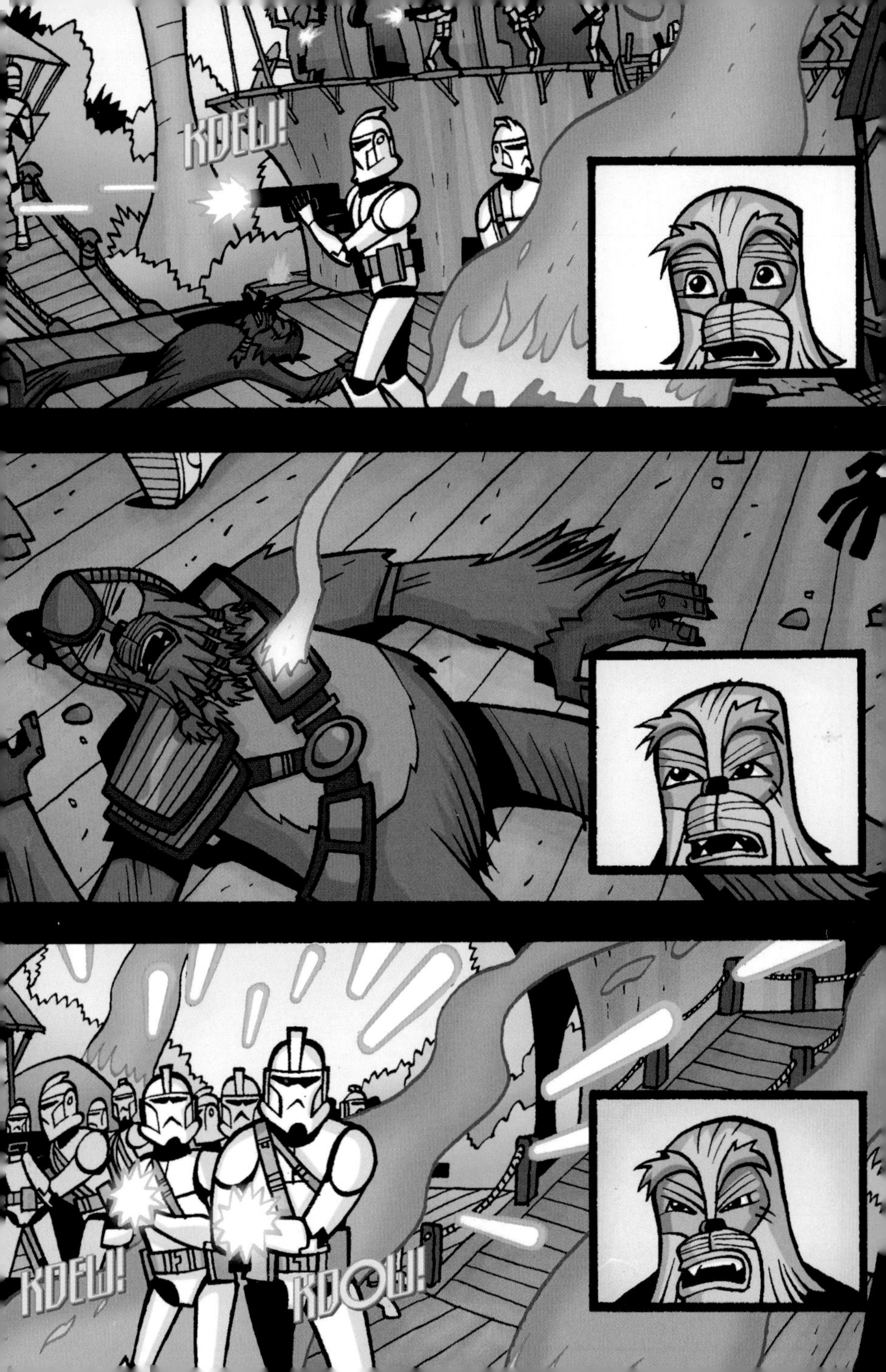
KDEW!
KDEW!
KDOW!

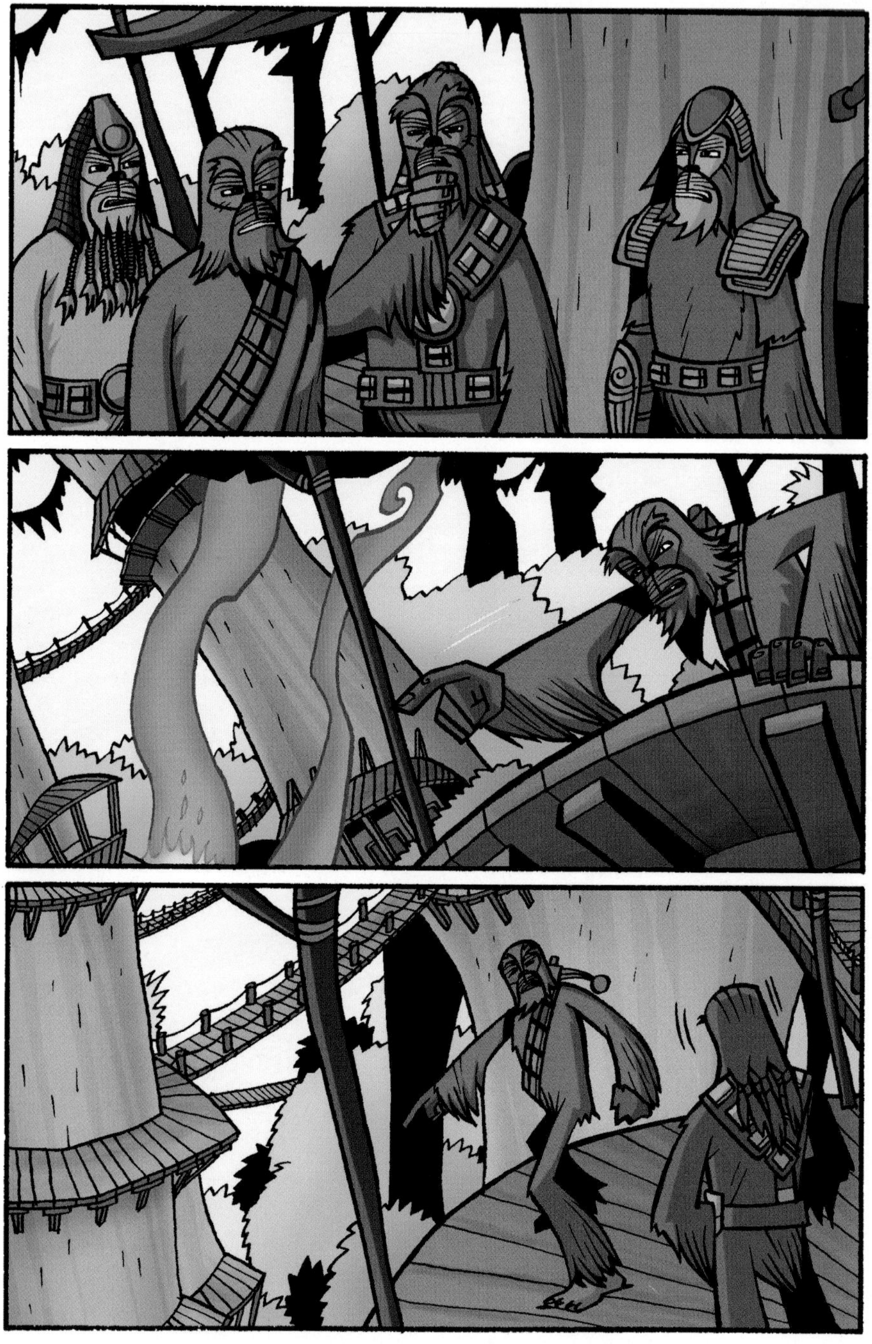

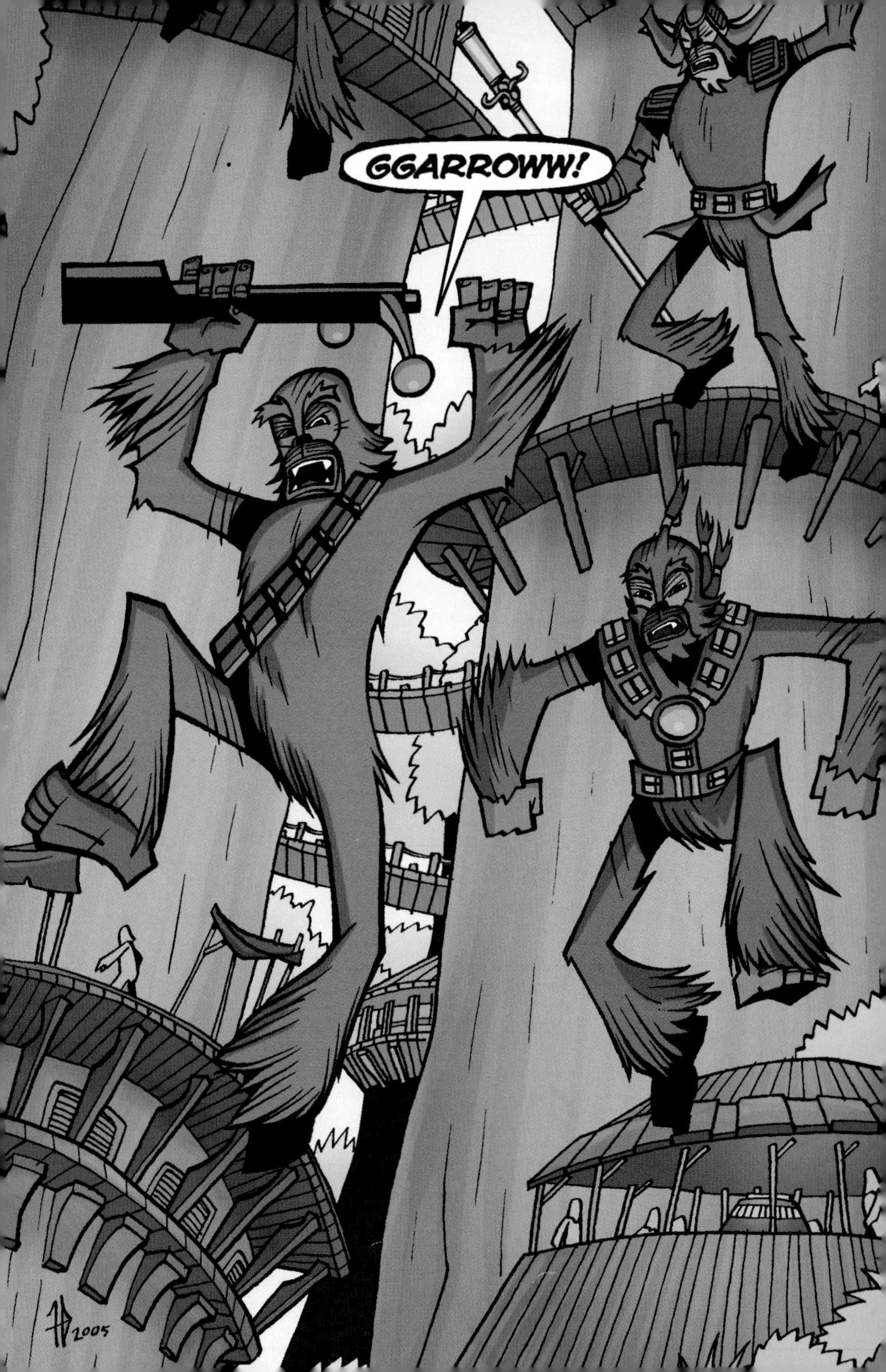
GGARROWW!

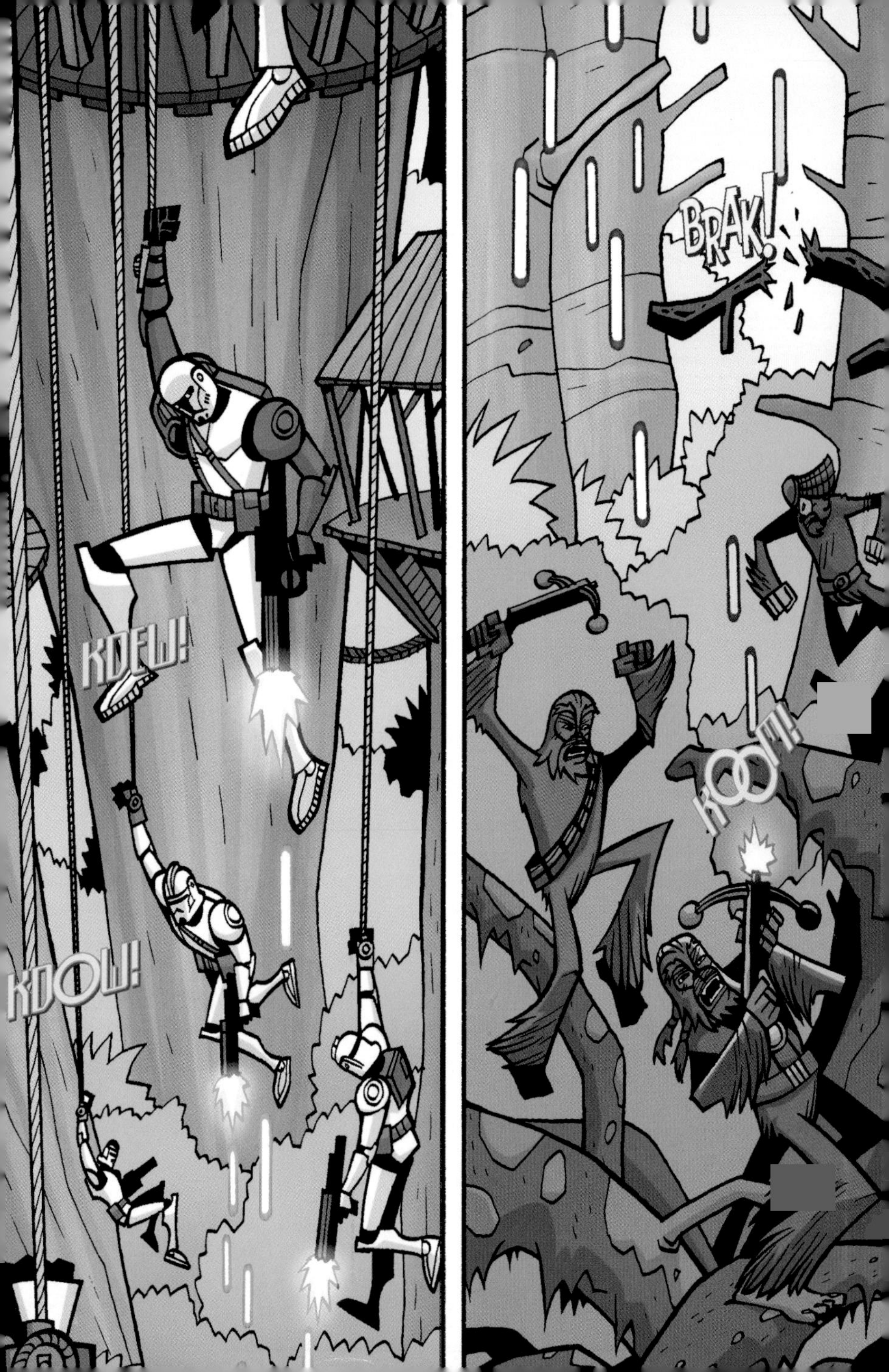
KDEW!
KDOW!
BRAK!
KOOM!

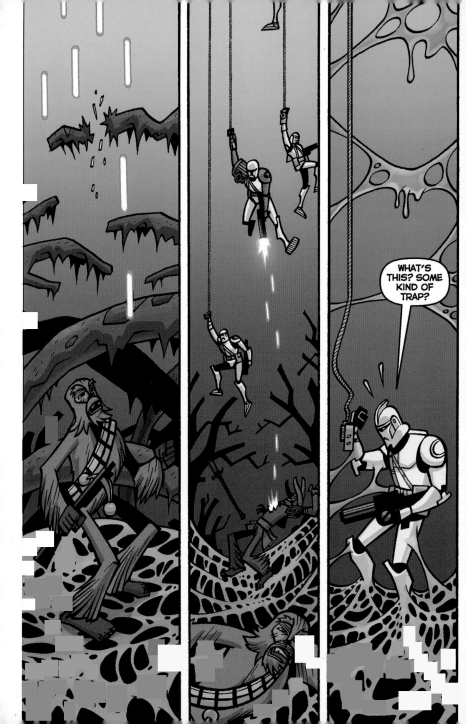

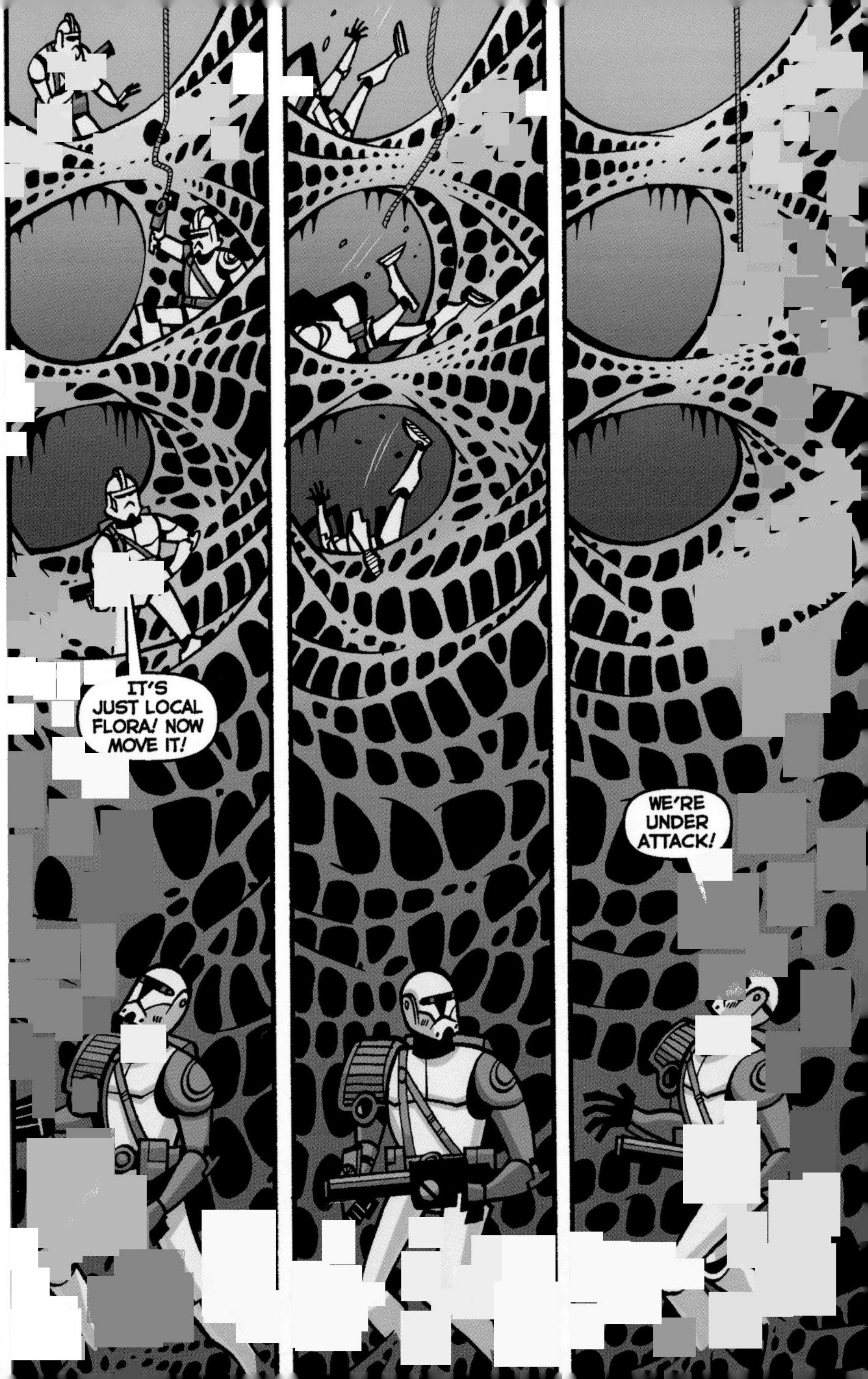
IT'S JUST LOCAL FLORA! NOW MOVE IT!
WE'RE UNDER ATTACK!

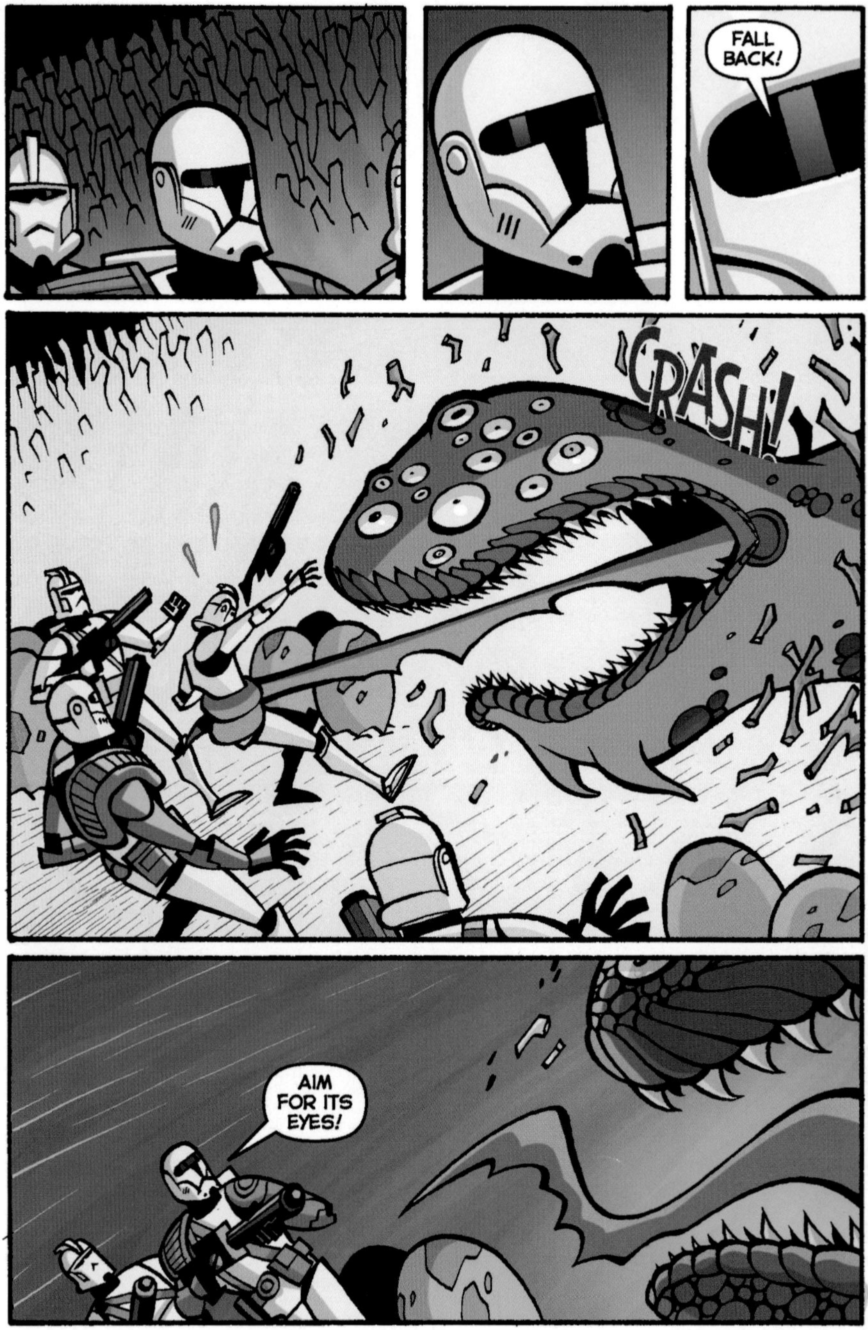
FALL BACK!
CRASH!
AIM FOR ITS EYES!

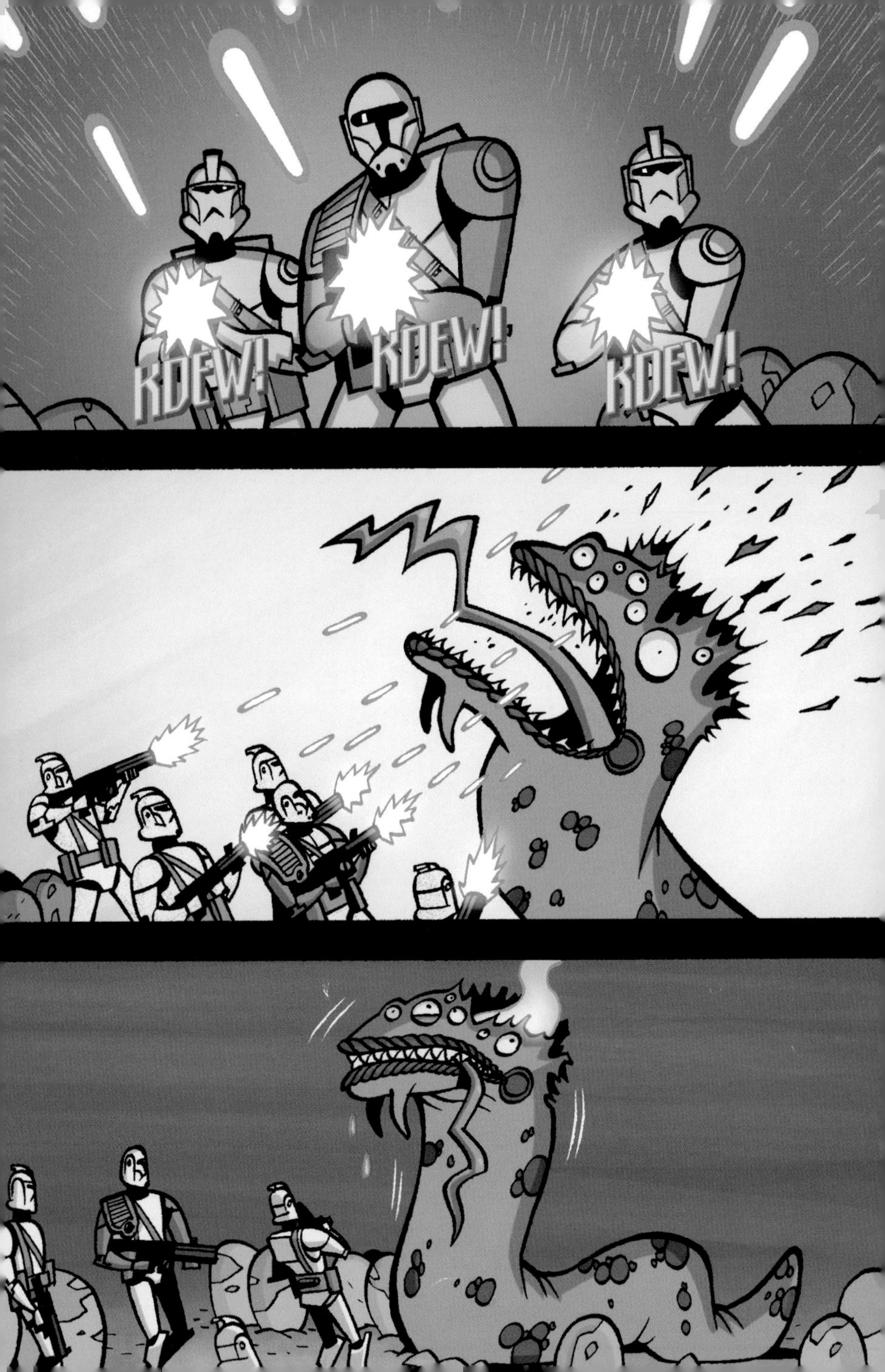
KDEW!
KDEW!
KDEW!

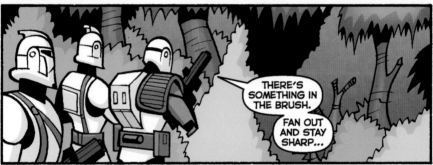

THERE'S SOMETHING IN THE BRUSH.

FAN OUT AND STAY SHARP...

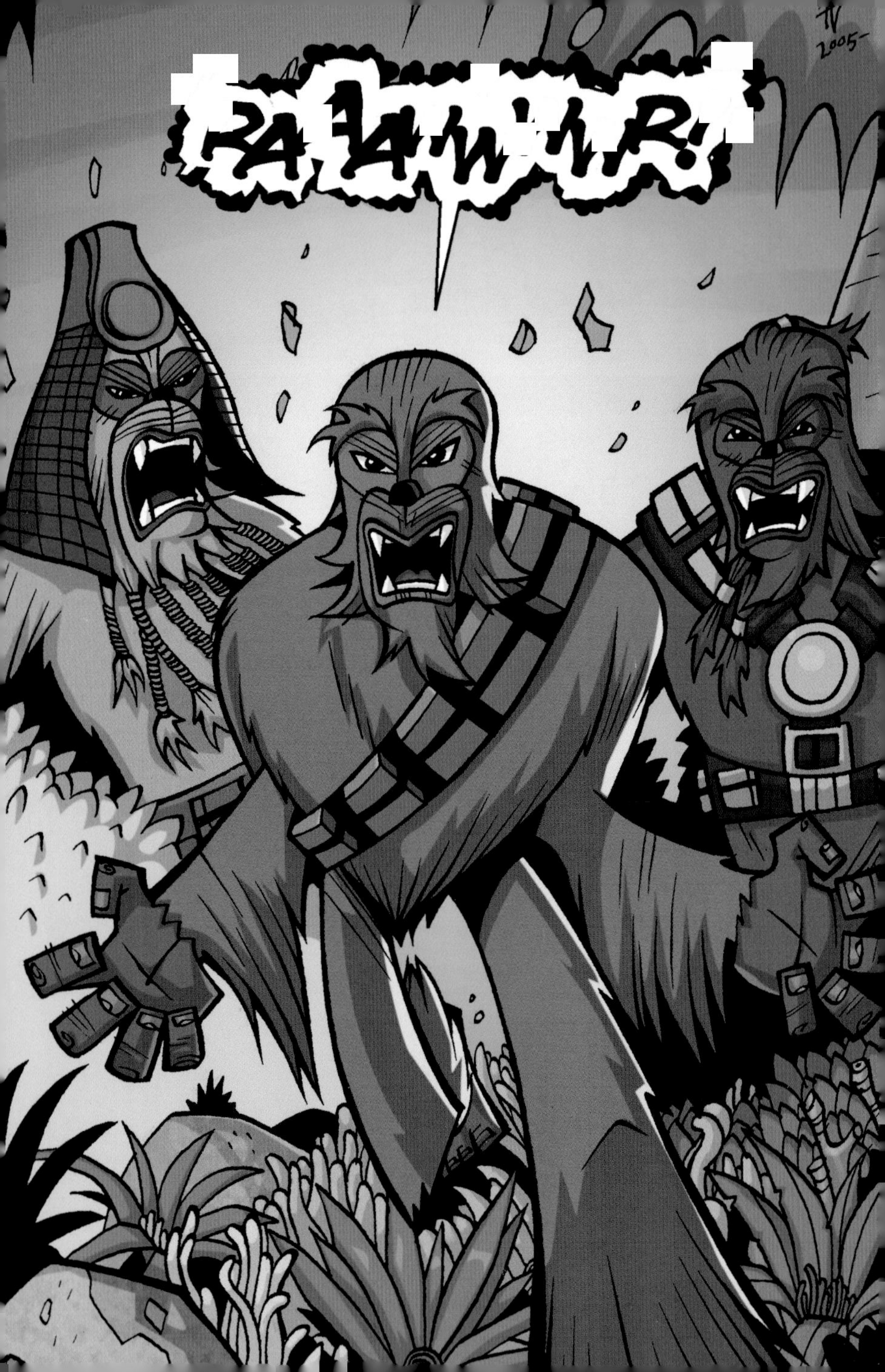
TV
2005

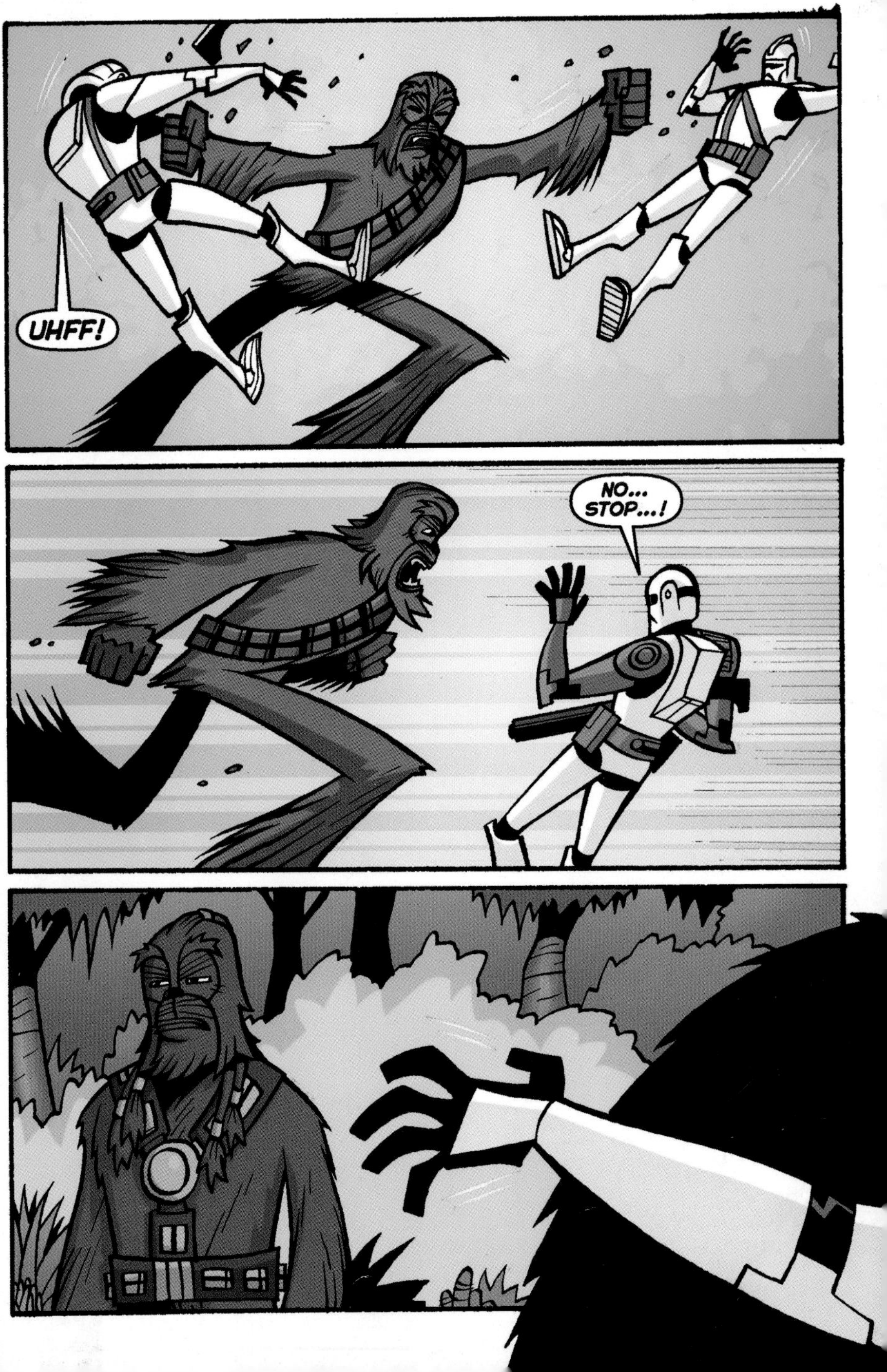
UHFF!
NO... STOP...!